Sanitarium Magazine
Issue no. 4

*Thank you to all of our
contributors, we
couldn't have done it without
you.*

Contents

ISSUE FOUR

Here we are, a few days away from saying goodbye to 2012 and what a 12 months it has been. Self-Publishing has had its up's and downs with review-gate, multi-book deals signed and new eBook readers entering the market just to mention just a few.

This issue of Sanitarium introduces 8 new writers, along with a couple who have graced its pages before. We have an interview with Carrie Green and we see "Where the Horror Happens" with Joe Mynhardt from Crystal Lake Publishing. Not to forget our Group Therapy session, top 10 bestsellers, your letters and as it is the Holiday season we take a look at some stocking fillers that you might have missed.

Looking forward to 2013, the obligatory resolutions will have been made, and some will be broken on the 1st no doubt. Until then keep writing, and sending in your submissions as there will be no stopping us in 2013.

With more features, interviews and masterclasses its a great time to be a horror fan.

BarrySkelhorn

Gasoline

Logan Edwards

Physician: Dr. Roundtree
8245-AVD12

"Bitterness is like cancer. It eats upon the host. But anger is like fire. It burns it all clean."- Maya Angelou

Ilove fire. I love the way it consumes all in its meandering years, as I recall when I was about three. I failed to realize the intense heat of the campfire my father built and I attempted to retrieve the glowing red coals strewing its edges. They burnt me. However, the incident branded my mind more than my hand with scars. I soon began experiments in my shed without the knowledge of my parents. How could I ever hope for them to understand my calling? I acquired many scars over the 12 years of tests I formulated in that corrugated, old shed. I miss that shed. It was about 7 by 7 feet, made of wood, with a corrugated metal roof. A single, bare light bulb hung from the ceiling, lit by an extension cord. My workbench was on the wall far from the door. A white tablecloth soaked in alum covered it. Several times, my pyrophoric mixes spattered in my face. The strength of my concoctions intensified as I entered puberty and found myself without female companionship. I finally burnt my laboratory down following the rejection of Sandra Delphino. I had so much to prove and so little chance to redeem myself. Girls were all hypocrites anyways, saying they wanted the best, but always choosing a boy who would never make it to college and give them the money they're all really after.

There was only one ray of sunshine in my existence, Artemis McCandles. She was a grade above me, part of the inner circle (the mean girls). I don't understand why she, unlike anyone else in the school, tolerated my existence. I loved the way her dark hair flowed down her back, a waterfall carved of brown glass. Her eyes were green. The scent of vanilla wafted behind her as she traversed the hallways. However, she had an odd habit of keeping her arms covered. I would shadow her throughout the school just to admire her lovely form. Of course, I was careful never to let her see me; that would drive her away. She must have taken pity upon me for her to consider conversing with me. As soon as she would try to include me in her dialogue, I would freeze and quickly affect an exit. Many times this occurred. On one lucky occasion, I found her away from her hawk-like friends, entering her vehicle. I steeled my nerves, approached her as if she were a live grenade, and asked if she would take me home. She turned to face me with a black eye. I asked if she ok and what had happened. She responded that she had fallen down the stairs. I knew she was lying, but I pretended to take her for her word and entered the car after she said yes. The ride home with her was sweet torture in its purest sense.

"So, Geoffrey, how was your day?" I got sick to my stomach as I staggered for a response.

"Good."

"Well, that's good, I guess. Uh." The conversation fell flat, but Artemis attempted to revive it. "I'm sorry my brother's such a prick to you" She was referring to her twin brother, Vincent, or Vince for short. He was a complete animal on the wrestling mat and a complete monster to me. I hated that dick; he treated me like trash. Every day, he'd leave a welt or bruise on me for his own personal amusement. That's the way high school goes though; one in-group person attacks an out-group person and the others swarm like bees, basic sociology. Except, I had no in-group to fight back with me.

"It's fine, the universe seems to have a way of dealing with people like that."

"If it helps, I don't care for him much either." Was there a quaver to her voice? Couldn't tell, but there was probably one in mine. "He's cruel and calloused, like my father." That was when it clicked. Her father was the one who gave her that black eye; I just knew it. It would all make sense, wouldn't it? Her brother probably learned it from him.

"Well, that's too bad, but I'm sure everything will turn out fine." I sat at her side for the few wonderfully tormenting minutes left before reaching my home. I muttered a farewell and hurried into my home.

After the crucible I weathered that day, I grew much more confident and started setting fires to commercial structures. My skills and research ensured that the police were at a loss for leads. No pattern, no warning, no evidence. Another wonderful thing about fire, it tends to dispose of the evidence for you. I used my above-average intelligence to get a hold of Artemis' address. I rode with Artemis again the next week, and was horrified to catch a glimpse under that sleeve. I saw one bruise, and I grabbed her sleeve and pulled it up before she could react. Her arm reminded me of a distended corpse. It was a nauseating painting of black, blue, green, and yellow on a pink canvas. Artemis looked back at me with shame. I faced forward and rode the rest of the way in silence. I knew what I had to do.

I headed for my basement, grabbing supplies I must leave out of this composition for safety's sake, and applied my pyrotechnic skill to an improvised explosive device. Haha! That beast thinks he has had the last laugh! The final joke would be on him, however. I examined the justice bringer for flaws, sprayed the creation down with an ammonia/Drano mix, and wiped it off to remove fingerprints and any stray DNA. The explosive had been concocted myself from non-assuming ingredients, meaning no federal bureau of investigation would trace it back to me. I knew her father's work schedule as well as I knew hers. My plan was so brilliant that they would never suspect me!

The following day, before school, I snuck to the vehicle of the demon and planted the tilt-fuse device next to the gasoline tank. I hoped the resulting conflagration would consume any evidence I had failed to dispose of. I smiled, knowing I would free my Valkyrie from her torment today. I retreated and made my way to Red Oak High for the day, sure I was unseen. I was high-strung the entire day and every time I heard my name mentioned, I jumped. I could not wait for the release of energy and demise of Mr. McCandles. I knew that Artemis would likely leave school or break down once she found out the news, and she would likely be the first to find out. I awaited this signal that entire day. To my dismay, the sign failed to materialize and I was in the dark. After school, I made a point of passing by her house. Her father's car was absent, so it may have failed to go off during school hours. I hurried home and awaited the news. I watched the local news and found that an exploding vehicle was never mentioned. I immediately headed for my basement, again, and began smashing all my supplies. My temper was as fiery as my passion. Mercury and gasoline mixed freely on the shag carpet when a flash of insight hit me.

In Artemis' backyard, there was a large oak tree facing her window. I had practiced climbing up the burnt-out tree in my own yard before I attempted to climb that behemoth. Once my skills had been honed to the level required to avoid broken limbs (trees' and my own), I walked out of my front door into the warm September night. My parents were too busy drinking and fighting to care about my exit. I evaded the roving police patrolling for curfew-breakers, hopped the picket fence, and landed as in Artemis's lawn. I grappled the tree and ascended the trunk faster than a chimpanzee. I perched myself on the third or fourth limb up and got a wonderful view of her bedroom. Artemis was sitting on her bed in a t-shirt and volleyball player's shorts apparently doing homework. I waited for her to prepare for bed. After what seemed like days, she moved from the bed to the dresser. She began to take her shirt off. Just as I thought she would reward my patience, an older man, her father, burst into the room and started shouting about some family affair. Artemis shouted back. Their voices trailed off and I couldn't figure out what they were saying. Her father said one last quip and left the room. Artemis resumed her routine when Vince entered the room and grabbed her arm. He said something to her and she shook her head back. Vince pinned her to the wall by her shoulders and positioned his face inches from hers. My hunch had been correct. Every fiber in my being cried out in rage and I wished to end his life. I barely avoided falling out of the tree in fury as he grabbed her arm and threw her on her bed. I stifled a yell as anger pierced my mind. I was helpless to affect the situation as he talked and struck her, however my mind was running scenarios like a supercomputer to put a fear of God in the fiend in front of me. I slid down the tree, unable to witness anymore. No one was going to hurt Artemis without answering to me.

I snuck to her father's car, almost the victim of my conclusion jumping, found the fatal flaw, fixed it, and attached it to Vince's. I hoped this would end tomorrow. In English the next day, sweat ran down my body and brow as an explosion shook the school. People panicked. They sent us home after they checked every car and the school. The police and fire marshal began their investigation. I would likely be a person of interest due to my public hatred of Vince, but motive isn't enough to rule out reasonable doubt. I watched the news later to confirm my kill. The news anchor began speaking.

"A vehicle exploded at Red Oak High School today. Police say that although there is major property damage, luckily, no one was injured." This complicated my day. Vince would now be paranoid, a trait likely to make you more apt to survive someone like me. I would also be suspected in the explosion and put under the magnifying glass. It was act now or forever hold my peace.

I gathered what tools I had left and packed them into my backpack. I next grabbed my cell phone and biked to the condemned apartment building I had been scoping out as my next target. A large steel pipe cut a hole out of the building, about five feet off the ground, an air duct, maybe. All I would have to do is remove the metal grating on the outside of it and I would have an escape route. I snuck through the hole I had cut in the chain link fence and headed inside of the unstable structure. I distributed the accelerant and made sure the other exits were impractical.

I called Artemis's house and, quite luckily, her brother answered. I told him what I had witnessed and what I thought of him. I belittled his manhood and told him my location. I sat in a rotted wooden chair and started drinking what alcohol I had left to dull the pain later. I played him well, I knew his pride would override his common sense and fear and he appeared outside the building some 40 minutes later, gun in hand. I crept into my position and called out. He walked into the main hall with such confidence, poor dumb bastard. I dropped the match and a line of flames cut him off from the exit. He was startled and dropped the gun, which landed in a hole in the wooden floor. That was sheer luck, had no idea that would happen. I crept out of the shadows into his view. Vince's eyes narrowed when he saw me.

"You're as much a bitch as my sister. You think she could ever love something as hideous as you?" I smiled, he may laugh right now, but in a half hour, give or take, he'd be burning in hell.

"Doesn't matter, Vince."

"I called the cops; they'll be meeting us here."

"Well, considering I've turned every exit into a campfire, I'd say the police wont make a difference."

"Where is the exit, before I beat your ass to a pulp?" I merely pointed at the inferno behind him. He shoved past me and found the other bonfires the exits had become. The fire was reaching the point of consuming the building. Burning wood and brick fell from the ceiling. The fire cast an orange, hellish glow. He ran about, seeking a reprieve for his life. I laughed, knowing my exit was secure. He forgot me in his haste to seek exit and I slipped away to the waiting air duct. I began climbing through the pipe of hot, jagged, twisted metal when a horrid realization hit me. I had forgotten to remove the metal grating from the other side.

The End.

No Guts, No Glory

Richard Anthony Dunford

Physician: Dr. Peterson
9268-WCT29

Ateenage Thug waits impatiently. Sat with outstretched legs beside a table in a police interrogation room; all on his Larry lone-some.

This thug, he's nothing but a kid in big boy clothes. Learnt how to be tough from music and movies. Considers his ASBO a medal of honour.

He's the cancer of society. Boiling over with hostility and attitude. Fresh bruises on his face and knuckles.

His motivation: boredom.

The air conditioning coughs and splutters. Four plain walls drenched in a sterile florescent light.

A middle aged Detective enters the room, saunters past the Thug, headed for a dormant steel folding chair. His hair hasn't seen a comb in years, his shirt's un-tucked and he has a tiny mustard stain on his top lip.

The Detective casually strolls over to the chair and sets it up across the table from the thug.

He takes a load off. Laid back to say the least.

Maybe he thinks he's down with the kids. Maybe he dresses up in women's clothes on the weekend. Who knows. Either way, around here… he's the man in charge.

The Thug eyeballs a crucifix, dangling from the Detective's neck.

The cross catches the light. Gleams and glistens amongst murky surroundings.

The Detective picks up on the Thugs stare and asks, "You religious?"

The Thug chews his lip. Doesn't dignify the question with a response. Glances around the soulless room as the Detective tucks the necklace under his shirt collar.

"Have you heard the story of the frog and the scorpion?" asks the Detective.

The Thug rolls his eyes and exasperates a laboured sigh of disdain.

"So this scorpion wishes to cross the river," says the Detective. "He encounters a frog and asks if he could ride on his back as he doesn't know how to swim. This frog didn't come down in the last shower and asks the scorpion 'how do I know you won't sting me during the trip?' The scorpion argues that if he did sting the frog while they crossed they would sink and he would drown. The frog accepts this logic and agrees to carry the scorpion across the river. They get about halfway across when the frog feels a sharp pain in his back. The scorpion has stung him with his lethal poison. The Frog looks up at the scorpion completely bemused. Asks him 'why have you stung me? Now we are both doomed.' The scorpion replies, 'I couldn't help myself, it's just in my nature!'

The Detective lets the words linger for a moment. Lets his young offender absorb them and draw meaning.

"Well if I knew I'd get a free story," snarls the Thug, "I would've got myself arrested long before now!"

The Detective can't help but smile as he flicks through the Thug's case file.

"You've had quite a night!" exclaims the Detective.

The Thug twists his head and spits on the floor.

The Detective is not amused. He glares at the youngster, demanding a verbal response.

"And?!" snaps the Thug.

The Thug sends him a sneer of contempt, itching for a confrontation.

The Detective isn't flustered; he's seen this type a thousand times before.

"Anything to say for yourself?" he asks.

"I want my phone call!" demands the Thug.

"Making a phone call won't change your life… but answering one!"

The Thug snorts, scrunches up his face. Decides to humour his foe.

"What are you talking about granddad?"

The Detective grins, a sudden gleam in his eye. The Thug has taken the bait. He has his attention.

The Detective leans on the table and looks deep into the young hoodlums venomous stare.

"A phone rings," the Detective begins, "Could be one of two callers. Caller one will make all your dreams come true, with just the click of a finger. Money, women, power. Whatever floats your boat... But, if caller number two is on the other end of the line... you're dead. Quick as a flash. No re-takes, game over. Fifty fifty chance. All or nothing."

The Thug ponders, intrigued. His wall of hatred showing cracks. Using his mind for something other then video games and searching for free pornography on the internet.

"So," prompts the Detective. "What would you do?" "Those are my only two options?"

"You've got a third… continue with your life as normal." "I'd answer the phone!" states the thug.

"You made that decision pretty quick." "Easy choice."

"Why?"

"No guts, no glory!"

"So you're a gambler?"

The thug smiles; a gloating smile.

"What if it's caller two?" the Detective challenges.

"Everyone dies eventually!" shrugs the teen.

"So you'd take that chance," the Detective continues. "To live like a king?!"

"Hell yeah" the Thug boasts.

"Really?! Swear to god you'd answer the phone?" "It'll kill me either way!"

His answer intrigues the Detective. Takes him off guard. He asks "How do you figure that?"

"If it's caller two," says the Thug, "I die instantly, no time for regrets. If I let it ring out the not knowing will slowly eat me alive. Only one way to find a happy ending."

"Interesting theory… I'm impressed. You're not as dumb as you look."

The Detective reaches under the table. Collects something… …a phone.

He places it smack dab in the middle of the table, pointed towards his young nemesis.

The Thug smirks.

"No guts no glory right?!" says the Detective.

The Thug is not amused, shakes his head in mock dismay.

The PHONE RINGS.

Startles the Thug. He Laughs.

The Detective's smile dissolves. Turns serious.

RING, RING.... RING, RING.

The Thug raises an eyebrow, not falling for the gag.

The Detective isn't joking, trains iron hard eyes on the
Thug. "Well," says the Detective, "Aren't you gonna
answer it?" "It's not for me is it!" the Thug replies.
"I have a feeling it is for you!"
The thug squints at the Detective, trying to read his face like
a poker player on a bluff. The Detective stays stoic, never
falters, doesn't even blink.
The Thug contemplates, glares at the ringing phone before him.
He reaches out. The Detectives eyes go wide as saucers, watching
like a hawk. The Thug meets his stare. His hand begins to
tremble.
RING, RING... RING, RING.
"What are you waiting for?" asks the Detective.
Beads of sweat form on the Thug's brow.
He bottles it; retracts his outstretched arm.
The phone stops ringing.
The Detective leans back in his chair. A rye smile props up
the corners of his mouth.
The Thug turns ruby red. Angry words rise in his throat but
he swallows them and bites his tongue.
The Detective stares at him, trying to read the thoughts behind
his eyes.
"This your idea of a joke eh?!" snaps the thug. "You pigs
get a good laugh out of that did ya?!"
The Detective's face goes passive. he shakes his
head. "So I'm gutless!" the Thug blurts out. "Happy
now?!" "Why are you getting upset?"
"Screw you man!"
The Thug sulks.
"Very few people would take that call," the Detective
reassures. "Not with their life on the line. It's one thing to say
it hypothetically, but in practice, that's a whole different
story."
The Detective stands and ambles to the door. A hint
of compassion for the cancer of society.
"I'll go fast-track your paperwork" says the Detective. "Sit tight."
The Detective leaves the Thug alone, still steaming from being
shown up. Annoyed with himself. Not so tough after all.
The PHONE CHIMES.
"You've got to be kidding!"

The Thug looks around, spots a CCTV camera mounted in the corner.

Yells out: "That's not funny!"

RING, RING… RING, RING.

The thug is about to answer the phone… but has second thoughts.

Can't bring himself to take the risk, just in case.

He crosses his arms and sighs.

RING, RING… RING, RING.

It's mocking him!

The thug has heard enough. He grabs the phone, rips out the chord and tosses it away.

The ring tone flat-lines and dies.

The thug mumbles 'stupid phone' as he sits back and stews. Only the sound of his tapping foot punctures the silence.

Then… THE PHONE RINGS!

The thug jolts backwards.

He gets to his feet, eye-balling the phone.

RING, RING... RING, RING.

The Thug paces to the exit. Tries the handle but it's locked. "Hey!" he shouts, "Let me out!"

He bangs his fists on the door and glares at the CCTV camera. No response. No reprieve.

RING, RING... RING, RING.

"Stop ringing!" he yells.

His mind racing. The walls caving in.

He holds his hands to his ears but can't block out the sound.

RING, RING… RING, RING.

A wave of determination washes over his face.

He storms towards the table. Reaches out for the phone...

... but stops himself at the last minute.

Curses the air. Hangs his head.

The phone keeps ringing. Teasing. Taunting.

The Thug wrenches the ringing phone from the table, lofts it high above his head and hurls it into the wall with all his might.

The phone smashes into a dozen pieces as silence fills the air. The Thug takes a moment to regain his composure. Turns back to the door and starts banging.

"Come on!" he bellows through the wooden door. "Get off your fat arses and let me out."

Components of the broken phone are sprawled all over the floor.

The individual segments start to pulsate.

Cogs and springs pulsate like jumping beans. Split wires coil and slap against the floor like a wish out of water.

The shattered pieces are drawn together by an invisible magnetic force and bind together, unbeknownst to the distracted Thug.

The dislodged cable slithers along the floor like a python and links up with the cracked shell.

The phone morphs, re-assembles and propels itself back onto the centre of the table. Damaged reversed. Good as new.

RING, RING... RING, RING.

The thug stiffens as a shiver runs up his spine. He slowly swivels to face the inevitable, the colour draining from his face.

RING, RING… RING, RING.

He can't believe his eyes. Hasn't blinked once.

Knows this isn't going to go away. Knows he has to answer. Takes measured steps of caution over to the table, sits back down, never taking his beady eyes off the ringing phone.

RING, RING… RING, RING.

He gulps down a ball of fear. Takes a deep breath.

No guts no glory!

The Thug snatches hold of the phone. Picks it up.

Presses the receiver to his ear.

"Hello?"

The End.

Smoke Break

Fallon Stoeffler

Physician: Dr. Edgar
9828-SJE41

"They have asbestos in them, did you know that?" Mary, (42, weight problem), points to Clarice's pack of menthol cigarettes, her own ultra-light clamped between two teeth. It quivers up and down as she talks, like the needle on a lie-detector test. Her lips are painted with smudged purple-red lipstick which leaves its sticky residue all over the filter part. You can tell which butts that litter the ground of the smoking area have been contributed to Mary by looking at the shriveled up filters.

Clarice, (39, prematurely gray) shrugs. She's a woman of few words, generally, and certainly doesn't usually waste them dignifying Mary's constant running social commentaries. She's out here because she wants to smoke cigarettes. It's cold and she doesn't particularly like Mary, a fact which, like most others, she holds close to the vest.

"Not asbestos, *fiberglass*," Mary corrects herself.

Sara, who says she is 35, making her the youngest member of their group, digs around in her own overnight bag-sized purse for her own pack. Sara always brings her entire purse down to the smoking area, keys, wallet and all, as if at any moment she's prepared to just take a run for it off the back closed in-patio of the 1970's office building and run across the field behind it. She continues to dig. "Damnit." She paws through the multitude of belongings with the devotion of a woman who knows that the clock is ticking on her 15 minutes of billable hours allotted for this quarter of the day.

Clarice wordlessly shifts her finger around her soft pack, manipulating the sticks inside until one slides up, and holds the whole pack toward Sara, who smiles gratefully at her as if she's just passed her a death-sentence pardon as opposed to a filtered Ultra-Light. Clarice notes again, as she has before, that Sara doesn't seem to have the problems the others do…that pesky business about aging. Behind Sara's back, on days when she doesn't come to work, they all play the number game…guess how many surgeries How many non-invasives?

The answer, truthfully, Is none. Sara has pale, soft skin, dark hair, good figure, and only the slightest hints of lines near the corners of her eyes.

"Thanks." She wastes no time in lighting up. Though she always digs for cigarettes in her gigantic purse, her lighter is always readily available in one of the pockets of her fitted, professionally-tailored pants.

Clarice just arches an eyebrow at her and goes back to staring at some unmarked spot on the plastic privacy fence behind Mary's head. She has her suspicions that Sara has no cigarettes at all in that big bag, and makes the grand show more often than not until someone just passes her one.

"What exactly do you keep in there?" Lisbeth Sullivan (37, brow lift, tummy tuck) asks her, staring. She's leaned up against one of the plastic vertical supports of the fence, her customary support position for smoke breaks. The ground around that particular spot is littered with the ends of the herbal cigarettes that she smokes.

There's a shrug. "I keep exactly what I need in here," Sara answers.

"Okay, that's a non-answer," says Lisbeth, and sulks back against the white pole. It's a cold day out and though she's wearing a scarf she could bundle around her neck a few more times, she doesn't , because that makes it smell like smoke. And she's not a big fan of the cigarette smoke smell, though she smokes half a pack a day of the clove cigarettes. "What exactly could you need out here?"

"I need what I need," she shrugs.

"Anyone else freezing?" Asks Clarice. It is the first time that she's spoken around them in a week.

"Not really," Mary blows out her words on a cloud of blue-gray smoke. It hangs for just a moment in front of her face, like a special effects smoke machine, and then dissipates as the wind blows through. "That office is just so fuckinghot." She says it like the adjective and its expletive modifier like they are one complete word, no break in between. Fuckinghot. She does it with all of her adjectives and their expletive modifiers. "I don't even want to drink coffee in the morning because it's sixteen-thousand fuckingdegrees at my desk."

The other three women all stop puffing for a moment, giving her assessment their full attention, and nod agreement, even though none of them do agree. Mary is a little more than overweight, a large contributing factor to her ability to acclimatize to any freezing cold environment and balk at anything warmer than seventy.

There is a kind of quiet loyalty on the smoke deck outside between them, born out of their symbiotic need to smoke in pairs or more and not feel bad about their fifteen minutes every two and a half hours. Inside the office, in the real world, they would normally never talk. If it wasn't for the finely honed nicotine addiction that they all shared, there would be no semblance of friendship and no feelings lost between any of them. It would just cease to be, their delicate bond.

Because of this they know the things about one another that the rest of the world doesn't. Clarice is divorced, and remarried, and her husband is having an affair with their au pair (that's what she calls it, like making it sound fancier takes the sting off of just saying that he's sleeping with their babysitter). Mary is 42, weighs well over two hundred and eighty pounds, and lives with her mother. Lisbeth has a suffering-artist boyfriend who has a drug problem and the occasional tendency to be mean to her.

And Sara….well, no one knows about Sara. She's only been with the company about eight months, is stand-offish to the point of rudeness, and as far as they know, her only complaint is that she can never find her cigarettes. At least, that's what they'd thought up until about a month ago, when Sara had told them about her unique "ability" and then invited them in on it.

Don't you want to be young and beautiful? She'd asked. Sure, yeah, they all wanted to be both of those things but the time for that had come and gone. No, Sara had assured them with the calm air of a man selling door-to-door vacuum cleaners, all they had to do was their part of it, and then they could be off – Italy, Spain, France. No one would find them. How could they, they'd all be looking for saggy, middle-aged, overweight, three characteristics which Sara assured them they could avoid being ever again. And all they had to do was gamble away their souls.

Out here, out in the cold, surrounded on three sides by white plastic eight-foot privacy fence and one side by brick, next to two HVAC units that cooled all of the 6,000 square foot office building, the code of loyalty is strong and formidable. If they'd never formed these tenuous bonds in the first place, they wouldn't be here, waiting for the end of the break.

Today there is more silence than usual. Once settled in to their customary places, they all just stand there and stare at each other, at the fence, at the ground. They avoid eye contact and just wait for the fifteen minutes to be over.

"Well," says Sara at minute fourteen, looking around at the other women and throwing her cigarette on the ground. "Are you ready?"

The others look up, look at each other for the first time. As always when it is time to go inside, there is a little reticence on all of their parts. But this time maybe a little more. It is Clarice that answers first, and in a way, answers for all of them.

"Ready."

They all look at her, the woman who has just condemned them all. Sara throws down her purse, takes her glasses off. Her bright green eyes intensify slightly, and it is then that they all see that the skin around her eyes is much more improved since the last time they took a good look at her. It is younger, smoother. The bit of chest that peers out at them from the neckline of her v-cut blouse is supple, way younger than the thirty-five or so years that she assimilates her personality into. There is a steam rising from her, as if her body was so warm that it is causing condensation around it in the cooling afternoon air.

"I don't know if I can do this," says Mary, and she is afraid. Sara turns her eyes on her. Little flecks of gold in the seem to burn bright, like embers in a fire, on a dark night. Mary feels a dull, strange pain behind her eyes, like she's being pierced there with a red hot poker. It's not a coercion technique. Not at all. It's more like a warning. Stop talking. We've already decided.

Mary shakes head, her hand braced on her forehead, as if she is trying to drive out the pain. She wants to be beautiful, young, but like this?

"It's already too late," says Sara, and her voice is now like that of a snake, low, hissing, sinuous. She's now their focal point, the rummaging-around-in-the-purse girl gone and some other more base creature replacing her. This always works, she knows, because deep down, humans, especially women, are more driven by how others see them, more than how they really are, their ability to do good things. It makes the painful process of continued youth, immortality easy. Find people to share the burden, relax a little bit.

Her next words cut through the air and seem to answer what they're all feeling, the cold feet, the last minute regret.

"Who cares about your soul," she says, "If you're going to live forever?"

They all leave quietly, their cars in the parking lot. They take public transportation and don't speak, knowing where they'll meet up later.

At Clarice's house they find her husband and his mistress, their au pair, stacked on top of each other like two fish at the bottom of a barrel. There is an archer's arrow spiked through both of them, pinning them together. The kids are at their real father' s house for the year, in luck due to their strange bi-yearly, bi-coastal custody agreement, don't have to see their step-father slaughtered in his own bedroom.

They've been exsanguinated.

At Mary's house, they find her mother, her insides opened up and splayed out all over her fifteen-year-old lazy boy recliner.

At Lisbeth's condo, they find her boyfriend in a crumpled pile at the bottom the stairs that lead up to the loft which is his "artist's studio," which is fancy terminology for the room that contains little else other than blank canvases, a fridge full of booze, hypodermic needles in the compartment where the butter should be. Like Mrs. Carruthers, the extensive damage to the rest of Ken Walter's body leads everyone's eyes off from the knowledge, at first, that he's been let of most or all of his blood.

At Sara's house, they find a perfect modernist kitchen, black granite countertops, white painted cabinets and stainless steel appliances and double sinks, spotlessly clean in the bathroom. They find a fridge, which contains nothing inside, room after room of grey painted walls and thin, steel-framed furniture and impeccably kept white berber carpets. In the master bedroom, they find a likewise rumple-free bed. On top of the covers, they find skin.

An entire human skin.

One of the investigating officers runs out of the room and throws up into the ceramic sink bowl, while his partner gapes.

"Where's the body? Where's the blood?"

"Wow," says one of the CSI that shows up. "Like a snakeskin." He loses his lunch then in the hallway.

On the back patio of the Regent Park office patio, they find full-body skins of the three other women. On the ground is a pack of ultra lite cigarettes, a pack of menthols, and a brown paper package full of clove cigarettes.

They've called her by many names: The Blood Countess Elizabeth Bathory was the one most renowned. She views herself as an opportunist. It is easy to stay young, healthy, beautiful. It only depended what – or who – you were willing to sacrifice. Blood for continued youth, renewal of womanhood.

On a stretch of beach in Italy, at the base of a cliff on the Amalfi coast, four young, beautiful women sit at water's edge, watching it lap at their feet. From bright red lips twirl smoke tendrils, twisting and turning up into the sky. Moonlight illuminates the features that are cut delicately into porcelain white skin. They smoke in silence together as the waves lap up around their feet.

The End.

The Pixie at The Side of the Road

Edward Vaughn

Driving down Highway 60 I catch the pixie in my
headlights. She has her arm extended, thumb pointing to the
sky. The classic hitchhikers pose. I speed past her then slam
my foot against the brake pedal. Pulling over I look in my
rearview mirror. The girl, painted blood red from the brake
lights, stares at my car. She picks up her backpack from the
ground and walks over.

Twisting in my seat I check her out. Skinny, but muscular
with perky breasts pushing
against her tight wife-beater. Green cargo pants hugging an
apple-shaped ass. Her blond hair cut boy short. It's what made
me think of a pixie. I press the unlock button. She opens the back
door, tosses in her pack, and gets into the passenger seat.

"Hey, thanks for stopping." she says.

"No problem. So, where are you
headed?" "Radcliff."

"That's a long walk."

"Yeah." she gives a bright smile, "Hence the hitchhiking."

"Ah." I say and pull back onto the road. "Sorry if this sounds
rude. But, has anyone ever told you that you look like
Tinkerbell?" "All the time." she says, "It's the hair. I just can't
stand hair on my
ears and neck, you
know?"

"Yeah, I hear you." I say. "You're such a pretty girl I'm sure
you would look good even
if you were bald."

"Well, thank you. That is so sweet. I could just eat you up."
She says, her smile getting
even wider. "Do you care if I
smoke?" "No, not at all."

She pulls out a soft pack of Marlboro Lights, a lighter with
a picture of a bat on it and
fires up a cancer stick. She takes a drag.

She blows a plume of smoke and says, "So, what's your name?"

"Michael. Michael Stein."

"I'm Penelope."

"Nice meeting you Penelope."

She reaches over to shake my hand. I grip her small hand in mine. I notice dirt caked

under her chipped red fingernail polish. With her other hand she places the Marlboro in her mouth. Her plump pink lips wrap around the filter, taking another drag. Penelope gets comfortable by putting her feet on the dash. Flip-flops cling to her slender feet, her toenails painted red. *Terrible shoes for hitchhiking way out here.*

My eyes turn back to the road. The headlights carve a path into the ink black night ahead of us. Country stars sparkle like glitter in the night sky. Smoke begins to clog the air so I press the window buttons down. Penelope tilts her head back as the wind rushes into the car, smoke sliding between her lips.

"Too much wind for you?" I ask.

"No, it's cool. I love the fresh air."

Out of my peripheral vision I can see her licking her lips. Not in a way to moisten them

because they're dry. More like a hungry animal wetting its pallet. Her tongue protrudes all of the way out of her mouth, touching her chin and sliding across her nose. I chance a quick glance but she stops. She stares out into the night, flicking ash out of the window. I rub my eyes. *Am I hallucinating? It's dark, I must be seeing shit.*

Penelope sniffs the air in a deep lungful as if smelling a delicious roast turkey. I look at

her and say, "You okay?"

"Yeah, I'm good. Just allergies."

"Oh. Got them myself. My sister's allergies were so bad as a kid she had to take

treatments."

"That's awful. I would hate to have to deal with that every day. Does she still have to

take treatments?"

"Naw, she grew out of it." I say.

The road continues to roll behind us. I change the conversation from my boring life to learn more about her. "So, where you from?"

"Around here. Meade County mostly."

She doesn't elaborate so I say, "I'm on my way home to Valley Station. Just left my

sister's house in Brandenburg. I bought a half-quarter from her boyfriend. You smoke?"

"Yeah, every once in a while." She says.

I search under my seat and pull out a Doral cigarette box. Flipping open the top I show her the contents.

"I rolled the whole thing up before I left. Take one and fire it up."

She slides a joint out and flicks her half-smoked cigarette out of the window. Sparking a

flame with her bat lighter she lights up. She takes deep draws of the sweet leaf, exhales. After a couple of hits she passes it over.

"Cool, man. Thanks." She coughs.

She hands me the bud I and take a few hits of my own. For the next few miles we smoke the joint down to a roach. My mind spaced out and body relaxed.

Penelope points ahead where the headlights cut into the dark. "Hey, there's a store coming up. Can you stop? I want to get something to drink."

Thirty seconds later I see the lights from the little country store. I pull into the parking lot and stop next to one of the two gas pumps. The store has a single wooden door with a square window. I can't see inside but the parking lot is empty.

"Be back in a second." Penelope gets out of the car and walks into the store. I watch her

narrow hips sway as she disappears behind the door. Staying in the car I decide to switch on the radio. Alice In Chains, 'I Stay Away', powers through the speakers.

'I Stay Away' is followed by a classic rock tune, then a fist pumping rock anthem, then

another song, and another. Penelope still hasn't come out of the store. My bladder felt like a water balloon ready to explode. We still had thirty to forty-five minutes before we hit Dixie Highway. I get out, lean against the car and piss my name against the asphalt. Still no sign of Penelope. *How long does it take to buy a damn drink?* Zipping up my jeans I head into the store to hurry her along.

I push the door open, scanning the interior of the store. As I step inside I slip on the floor and grab a metal rack full of chips and candy for balance. The floor is completely wet. The clerk lies slumped over the counter facedown. Liquid drips off the edge of the counter and pools on the floor. *Spilled soda maybe?*

"Hey buddy. You see a girl come in here?" I ask.

The clerk doesn't move. I step closer. The liquid doesn't look like soda. It's too thick and too dark.

I touch the guys shoulder to try and wake him. He slides to the floor behind the counter.

"Holy shit."

There's a splatter of blood on the wall behind the counter. Rivulets racing down, heading for the cigarette cartons sitting on the shelf. I quickly back away and sprint outside. Sprinting around the rear of the car I glance over my shoulder at the store, hoping whoever did that isn't still around.

Getting into my car I slam the door shut. Penelope sits in the passenger seat offering me a 20 oz. bottle of soda. "I got this for you."

"What the fuck? Where were you?" I say, "That clerk in there is fucking dead."

"Really?" she says, a frown on her face. She glances toward the store as if she had never seen it before. "He was okay when I went in." She takes a healthy swallow of her Cherry Coke.

"Trust me lady. He is dead. There was fucking blood everywhere."

I start the car and push the pedal flat against the floorboard. Without looking I pull onto the highway, squealing tires.

"I need to find a phone. My cell is dead." I say. Sweat pours down my face. "We need to call the police."

Penelope sits next to me cool as a polar bear's dick. She says, "Pull over onto this road."

"What?"

"Pull over."

"I told you, we have to call the police." I say.

Penelope grabs the steering wheel and turns the car onto the shoulder of the road. I stand on the brakes.

"What the hell is wrong with you lady?" I throw the car into park.

Penelope grabs me by the throat with both hands. The pupils of her eyes have shrunk to periods. Her jaw opens twice as wide as it should. I can hear the bones in her jaw break and realign. The corners of her mouth tear all the way to her ears. Blood speckles my face.

She bares shark-like teeth with rows of jagged spikes. My mouth hangs open in a silent scream. Saliva and blood drain into it and onto my cheek, in my eye.

I instinctively put my hand against her chest and shove her to the other side of the car. I grab the door handle and spill out onto the ground.

The passenger side door explodes from the car. Crawling on all fours Penelope steps into

the headlights. Her knees are now bent the opposite direction they should be. Teeth gnashing, drool and blood spilling at the corners of her mouth.

She no longer looks like an adorable pixie. She looks like a demon from the bowels of

hell.

The sky begins to turn a yellow-ish orange. I sit on the ground unable to move as she slowly stalks toward me. She places her hands on my chest, nails like ice picks scratching me. Her face pushes close to mine. I feel urine soaking my pants as she growls in my face.

Dragging me by my shirt she takes off running toward the woods about a hundred yards away. The sun begins to crest the hills in the distance, burning away the coolness of the night. I dig my heels into the earth and rip grass out of the ground. My shirt tears in her grip.

I quickly scamper to my feet and run for my car. Twenty yards before I reach the car she slams into my back. My face bounces off the hard dirt, busting my nose open. Blood pours into my mouth and off my chin. I feel sharp needles stab into my back muscles, hot breath rushes into my ear canal. It smells like road kill on a hot summer day. She flips me onto my back. A wet tongue slides across my jaw and into my mouth, a morbid French kiss. I gag as it passes my uvula.

She licks the blood seeping from my broken nose. Close to my face she inhales deep. Her

razor sharp teeth sink into the top of my shoulder.

I scream.

The pain is unbearable. I feel warm liquid drench my shirt. The glittering sky begins to spin and I start to black out.

Suddenly, she lets go of me and scampers backward looking at the sky. The world slides into focus. I turn to where she is looking. The morning sun hovers above the silhouette of hills, bathing the valley in warm light.

Penelope stands on her hind legs and screeches into the oncoming dawn. She turns and runs off toward the distant tree line, smoke trailing off of her skin. In a matter of seconds she zigzags the open field and disappears into the woods. I stay on my back staring at the sky. Finally, I roll onto my side. With my one good arm I push myself to my knees and crawl toward the car. My other arm drags a trail in the dirt behind me.

I reach the car door and open it. My fingers curl around the steering wheel. With all of my might I pull myself into the seat. I sink into it, all of my strength gone. The blood continues to soak my shirt and pools in my belly button. I start to feel light headed and my body won't stop shaking. I can't tell if it's the loss of blood or the adrenaline wearing off.

I stare into the oncoming day, in denial of what I had just witnessed. Somehow I manage not to pass out from the blood loss. I reach under my seat and pull out the box of joints. The bat lighter is still in the passenger seat. I take it and fire one up. I glance toward the rising sun, seeing it in a whole new light.

The End.

Crossroad

Marie Robinson

Physician: Dr. Lichten
6428-SED41

Westhouse the Wanderer threw back his head and, tipping the mug, he dumped the remaining ale into his mouth.

"Aaahhh…" he sighed, wiping his chin with the back of his wrist. He shoved a hand down into his coat pocket, fishing around until it reappeared clutching three coins. He placed the coins down on the counter, tipped his hat, and with a wink rose from the stool.

He was a very odd-looking man, particularly because of his wardrobe, which gave him the look of a clown who drunkenly wandered his way from the circus. His cap—which he tipped at every single person in the tavern on his way out—was of the tall top hat kind, covered in holes with a tattered blue ribbon tired around the brim. His clothes were shabby and mismatched patterns, his hands wore gloves with the fingertips cut off.

He was called Westhouse the Wanderer because he walked from place to place, never staying anywhere for long. He preferred to amble along the open road; see the splendors of nature—or so he claimed. In reality he was just a homeless man, but it made life more enjoyable when he viewed it that way.

Westhouse left the tavern and stumbled down the town road, where a woman was going along and lighting all the lanterns. The sky was blushed and the sun had not yet sunk, it was a bright red bulb sagging on the horizon.

The Wanderer tipped his hat at the woman as he passed. "Well, I've come through but now it's time for me to move along again." The woman stared at him and said nothing. Her eyes were wide and her gaze piercing like a cat's. She carried a small candle in her hand, which she used to light the lanterns.

"Lovely town, though," Westhouse added.

"Thank you," spoke the woman. She reached up to the lantern and opened its little glass door, holding the candle to the lantern's wick until it caught and grew a long, calm flame.

Westhouse held an arm out and pointed down the road. "Do you know these roads well?" He asked.

The woman gave a small nod. "You'll come to a crossroads about two miles down, and there you'll have to decide which direction to go. North, South, West, or East."

"Well, which would you recommend, ma'am?" He asked sweetly.

"I recommend that you be very careful on those roads at night, sir," she said gravely. "These twisted woods harbor some very strange things in them. Would you like me to lend you a candle to take along with you?"

"Oh, no, no, no," Westhouse chuckled, waving a filthy hand at her. "I've been a wanderer for too many years to be scared of the dark, miss. I thank you for your kind thought. Goodnight, now."

The woman watched him as he stumbled away, passing all the houses until the road was lined with only tall grasses. She whispered a prayer under her breath for him, and then rushed off to light all the lanterns before the sun went down.

***

Westhouse didn't notice the sun vanish, or the night appear. He didn't notice the trees darken and thicken as the light waned. He didn't even notice his own feet ambling along, until he came to the crossroads.

He stood in the center, his drunkenness finally faded to a small burning behind his forehead. He looked down each end of the road, and each end, unraveling into shadows, appeared the same.

As he looked around, Westhouse the Wanderer noticed a figure standing on the edge of the road. He was leaning on a long stick and wiping at his brow with a cloth.

Westhouse tipped his hat as he approached. "A fine evening, wouldn't you say?"

The man spat on the ground and raised his face to meet with Westhouses'. "I s'pose." He said gruffly. He was a somewhat young man, with fluffy brown hair and two beady eyes, settled closely together on his face. The stick he was leaning on was actually a shovel, its blade buried into the dirt. The man looked as though he was preparing himself for a task, set to take place under the fresh moonlight.

Westhouse stopped before the man and extended his hand. "Westhouse the Wanderer."

The man shook his hand and grumbled, "Bates."

Westhouse nodded and grinned. He rocked on his legs, rested his hands on his hips and nodded again. "I must say, whatever job you are about to do you're darn smart for puttin' it off 'till night. It just makes a labor that much worse performin' it under the burden of the Southern sun."

"Indeed," said Bates. "This is night work. You say you're a wanderer, eh?"

"That's right," Westhouse stated proudly. "Couldn't be anything else if I tried."

"Seems like it would be hard to come by cash with that occupation, unless you pick it off the side of the road. I'd give you your share if you wanted to lend me a hand."

Westhouse's heart buzzed. Even if the man was mocking him, he had a point; it was hard to come across money or kindness, and here he was offered both. He nodded his head so hard his hat bobbled round on his head.

Bates bent down and picked a second shovel off the ground that Westhouse had previously failed to observe. He held it out and Westhouse took it by the handle.

"Dig within these stones," said Bates, pointing down to the ground where a ring of stones were placed.

"All right," Westhouse agreed and readied the shovel in his hands. He brought it down and made the first strike in the earth. The ground was soft and gave easily to the spade.

The stones made up quite a sizable area on the ground; Westhouse noticed now that the shape they lay in was more like an oval than a circle. It was long enough that if he were to lie on the ground he would fit comfortably within it.

"It's quite dark," Westhouse noticed as he dug. The earth and the darkness blended together so that he couldn't quite see the hole he was digging, he was just pressing his shovel down into the squishy dirt.

"The moon shades its eyes on a night like this," Bates spoke solemnly. The whole time he had never once picked up his shovel, he had just stared down at the ground with a strange look in his eyes. Their gray centers were flecked with sorrow, longing, and a hint of madness.

"I'm sorry to be telling you this," he said finally, "but the hole you're digging up is a grave."

Westhouse paused, pulling the shovel from the earth and letting it rest at his feet. The dark hole gaped up at him.

"Who's grave is it?" Westhouse asked cautiously.

Bates sighed. "It's my wife's. "

I'll tell you the story," he said, laying down his shovel and crouching to roll a cigarette. "It's only fair. You're free to leave any time you want. However," he shot a stern look up at Westhouse, "you'll only get the coin if you see it to the

end." Westhouse gave a silent nod.

Bates lit a cigarette in his mouth and then handed it to Westhouse, who took it, and inhaled it as Bates' strange story began to unravel.

"Three days ago my dear wife, Sweet Alice, died." He shook his head, taking a long drag of his cigarette. "It was much before her time, I could tell just looking down at her darlin' face. It was so pale, as if a snow had settled over her skin; every feature frozen in time. She was too young and beautiful to die."

"How did she die?" Westhouse inquired from the other side of the grave.

Bate's face tightened, his jaw clenched. "Killed at the hands of a man. I just knew that her life had been taken earlier than it ought to, and I couldn't rest—couldn't do nothin'—until I made it up to Sweet Alice."

He looked back over his shoulders for a moment, casting his eyes down each long dark end of the road.

"I've always heard that crossroads were a strange place," he continued. "I've been told that by night they become the playgrounds to spirits, gypsy's, and demons. So, the night of her untimely death, I came to these very crossroads, dropped to my knees and called out to any creature that would listen.

"As I lay on the ground, weepin' into my hands, I heard a sound comin' down along the road, headed right for me. It was a carriage, drawn by a magnificent black horse, all muscles and mane.

"At first I had the idea to just let it trample me, and join my Sweet Alice at once, but the carriage slowed to a stop before my crumpled body. I rose to my knees and peered 'round the enormous horse, but I found that no one was holding the reins.

"I looked up strangely at the stallion, who was in turn staring down at me with black eyes, shining like marbles.

"As I was gaping up, speechless and still, it opened its mouth and began to talk. 'Speak what you want or get off the road.'

"I gasped, trembling at the hooves of the great beast. 'My wife,' I stammered. 'My wife is dead.'

"'All things must die,' spoke the horse in a deep, grumbling voice.

It sounded cavernous, ancient, and powerful.

"'No! It was before her time!' I pleaded. 'It was no natural death! It was…' I choked on the words, 'murder.'

"He told me that there was only one thing that I could do, but it was no ordinary task. I assured him I would do *anything*. "He said, 'You must bury her here, at the crossroads, in an unmarked grave, and there she must lie for three days. On the third night, you will unearth her, and she will be just as alive as you so fondly remember her.'

"I wept and thanked him over and over, finally rising to my feet.

Even at my full height the horse towered over me.

"His eyes were two unmoving black beads. 'Open the carriage door and get to work.'

"I did as he said, going to the carriage hitched up behind him. I opened up the door and seated inside was my Sweet Alice! She was slumped to the side, her eyes closed, just as beautiful as I remembered her. Except… there were dark rings around her neck, black bruises that encircled her lovely little throat. I cursed the hands that made them."

***

Westhouse the Wanderer still had the long extinguished cigarette hanging from his mouth; the shovel gripped in his hand; but there he stood motionless, his face gone white.

He plucked the cigarette from his mouth and tossed it on the ground. He looked upon Bates' face with wary eyes. "You know that all sounds… crazy, right?"

Bates chuckled, nodding his head. "Oh, I know. But, if you were given a once in a lifetime chance, wouldn't *you* take it? Wish-grantin', talkin' horses ain't somethin' that happens everyday. Don't you have a love of your own that you might save from the cold dirt of the grave?"

"No," said Westhouse shortly. "Wanderers don't have time for lovers." He hung his head, casting his eyes down into the pit. A pang of loneliness shot through his chest, and then vanished, like a strike of lightning.

"I'm afraid I must press on," he said finally, tipping his hat to Bates. "Goodnight, sir."

"No, no," Bates said, waving a finger, "I said you would only get the coin if you saw it to the end."

"Payment won't be necessary, I really must go." Westhouse the Wanderer made to leave, but Bates put a hand on his shoulder and looked up into his eyes. "I'll double it," he whispered harshly. "Stay and help me and I'll double the coin I was going to give you before."

"That won't be necessary, friend."

"Triple," Bates' bloodshot eyes burned as if lit by some unseen flame, his face was covered in sweat. He reached down to his pocket and shook it; it jingled like a chorus of little bells.

Westhouse's skin was creeping with uncertainty, his head was buzzing with worry, but he tried to keep his eyes and his voice cool and still. He gave a short nod, "All right."

***

"Somethin' doesn't seem right," sighed Westhouse, thrusting his shovel into the dirt. He paused a moment to wipe the sweat from his brow. "How come this thing is doing you a favor but asking nothing in return? It just doesn't seem right to me."

"There was one more thing it told me," Bates said, crouching to roll another cigarette. "It said to bury her with no coffin, just skin on dirt. So be gentle with that spade, because you're getting close." A chill ran through Westhouse's blood. He paused—he was deep down in the ground now. Sighing, he tossed his shovel back and got down on his knees and started clawing at the dirt with his hands.

"You're a good man, Westhouse the Wanderer," said Bates up above.

Westhouse grumbled and kept digging. He didn't even care about the coin anymore, he just wanted to be done with this and be on his way. He wouldn't mind forgetting it just as soon.

He snatched his fingers back as they brushed something cold and smooth just beneath the surface of the dirt. Westhouse remained frozen a moment, his heart beating fast in his chest. Forcing his quaking hands to move he reached back down and resumed wiping away the dirt from the snowy white face of a woman.

Once he had uncovered the entirety of her face—the eyes and lips gently shut—he couldn't help but find loveliness in the corpse.

He pulled the dirt away from her throat and whipped his hands back, his whole body going rigid with horror as he saw the dark rings that trailed around her neck like tight black chains.

"Mr. Bates," he called hollowly, "I found her."

Bates sprung to the side of the grave, looking down with a cigarette hanging from his mouth.

"Oh, my," Bates said dreamily. "She's even lovelier than I recall."

Westhouse pulled his hat from his head and laid it over his chest as he looked down upon her. Sweet Alice.

"Westhouse, you've been a wonder. I really don't know how I could have done it without you," said Bates, grinning down into the grave. He flicked his cigarette off into the night. "There's just one more thing I need you to do before we're through."

"What's that, sir?" Westhouse asked uncertainly.

"I'm gonna need you to lift the dear lady up and hand her to me. Can you do that?"

He looked down at Sweet Alice, and with a strange emotion in his chest (he could not tell if it was grief or love) he slid his fingers through the dirt, underneath her head and raised it up. Slowly, her body was pulled from the ground like the clinging roots of a lily. Westhouse held her slight frame in his arms, draped in a gown that he imagined was once as white as her skin, but now it was a drab gray, stained from the soil.

"There you go, now hand her up," said Bates excitedly. He held out his arms to receive her.

With one last long look at the girl, Westhouse began to lift her towards the night sky. As she rose, Westhouse felt a sudden warmth stir in her dead skin, and he saw the fingers on her hand, hanging from her limp wrist, begin to twitch. When she reached the arms of Bates, and a harsh gasp escaped the lady's lips. Her eyes fluttered open as Bates cradled her against his chest.

Westhouse shuddered, backing against the walls of earth as he looked up towards the moonless sky, where the corpse he had just dug out of the ground was catching her breath.

"Oh, darlin'!" Bates cried, tears slipping from his eyes as he leaned his head down to place a kiss on her lips.

"Get your hands off me!" Sweet Alice shrieked, squirming out of his embrace. She stood on her bare feet, the serenity of death lost from her face—it was now twisted in rage. She brought her hands, which were encased in lace gloves, up to her face, placing one on either side of her chin and her head a swift jerk to each side, her neck cracking grotesquely with each motion. She sighed, "Much better."

"Sweetheart, what's wrong?" Bates moaned, reaching out for her. "Come here, I've missed you!"

Sweet Alice shook a long white finger at him. "Don't think just 'cause I been *dead* don't mean I don't remember nothin'. I know what you done, and I *know* who put these rings 'round my neck!"

Westhouse the Wanderer watched the strange scene in horror from the bottom of the grave. He wished for daylight—even moonlight—to save him from the suffocating darkness.

"Darlin', you don't know what you're saying. You just woke up from the deepest of sleeps!" Bates chuckled, inching towards Sweet Alice with a hand outstretched.

She jumped back and shouted, "Keep those rotten hands away from me." She winced, reaching up and cupping her throat with a delicate hand. "It still hurts! Damn you!"

"Sweetheart, I don't think you understand the situation, here," Bates stammered. "I just brought you back to life! Don't you think that is worth some gratitude?"

With these words her face changed; her eyes rolled round to look off somewhere into the sky, and she mumbled to herself dreamily, "Back to life..." she nodded. Her anger washed away and she seemed to withdraw into her thoughts. "Yes... being dead is strange—well, I suppose I was only half-dead. I could hear the worms tunnelin' through the earth; the shovel turnin' up the dirt... and then I felt his wretched fingers on my face!" She spat, pointing down at Westhouse.

He blushed, crouching down deeper into the hole, his shivering fingers sinking into the mud.

Sweet Alice shuddered, wrapping her arms around herself. "Oh! It was so cold down there. It *is* nice to be alive again..." she turned her big eyes on Bates, who was clinging to her every word.

"Well, it sure is wonderful to have you back on this beautiful, still night. You look just as lovely as ever," Bates said sweetly.

"Oh, Bates!" Sweet Alice cried, throwing herself into his arms. She sighed. "It's nice to breath again, I felt like the dirt was creeping down my throat the whole time I was down there." Her glare snapped like a whip up at Bates. "Why'd you leave me down there so long?"

"Because, sweetheart, that's what the devil done told me to do," he answered matter-of-factly.

Sweet Alice pouted and laid her head back on his chest. "Well, let's go home, darlin'. I'd like to sleep above ground tonight."

"Of course, sugar. We just got one more thing to do before we go."

Bates put Sweet Alice under his arm, walking her over to the edge of the grave. He peered down into it, at the man who shook like a mouse in the corner.

"Westhouse, you're a smart man for bein' nothin' but a 'wanderer'," said Bates, a sinister grin sprawled on his face. "And a handy one, too. Look at this lovely hole you've fashioned!"

"Yes, sir," Westhouse muttered meekly, his face drenched in sweat. "Could you give me a hand to get out?"

"Well, there is one more thing I wanted to discuss with you." Bates placed a kiss on the head of Sweet Alice. "I wasn't all the way honest with you earlier—but I knew if I was you wouldn't help me out! I *am* mighty grateful for you helpin' me out. Sweet Alice might not act like it, but she's mighty grateful, too.

"Now, you mentioned there being a *catch* to this whole deal, and I have to tell you now, my friend, that there *is* one. That big ole horse told me that my Sweet Alice could have her heartbeat again after three days in the ground on one condition. And that is that the grave remained filled after she had rose out of it. I mean, think about it—a grave with no body in it, well that ain't no grave at all! That's just a lonely hole in the ground, servin' no use. So, make yourself comfortable, Westhouse, because you've just dug your final resting place."

Westhouse's blood froze; he sprang to his feet and turned to face the wall of earth. He extended his arms and fingers and jumped, reaching for the edge but falling just short. He clawed at the dirt, trying to lift his feet onto it to climb, but they only slid back down.

"Oh, come on now, it ain't so bad," called Sweet Alice from above. "'Course, I was only in there three days—you gon' be in there forever!" She placed a gloved hand up to her lips, stifling her laughter at first, and then she threw her head back and cackled wildly, the black rings stretched across her white neck.

Bates picked up his shovel once more, and walking to the pile of dirt that Westhouse had turned up earlier, he filled the blade with earth and tossed it back into the hole.

Westhouse began to scream, and the grave began to fill; Sweet Alice continued to howl at the moonless sky, and the shovel crunched as it dipped into the dirt.

***

Long after the dirt was packed, and the crossroads were empty, and the moon had advanced from behind her veil of clouds, screams still rung out beneath the ground, until the earth began to creep into Westhouse's mouth, filling it until silence was restored in the unmarked grave.

The End.

The Legend of Old Man Winsor

Andy Fish

"Hot as hell. A phrase the men used to describe that day. They were just a handful of American men, most barely over eighteen, in the south pacific going from island to island doin' their duty, or as they would describe it 'Buncha true blue Amer'can heroes killin' some goddamned Japs in the shittiest parta hell.' Among them was Private Charles G. Winsor, a nineteen-year-old kid straight outta high school.

He and his twin brother, Max, both enlisted the day after they graduated. Max went off to France where he was shot and killed by a ganga Nazis, and Charles was sent to the Pacific front where he managed to survive. Yes, Private Winsor lived through many days of battle largely uninjured, but on that day, the one when all the men said "it's hot as hell today", somethin' horrible happened.

They landed on the little island and crawled through the dense jungle just as they always did. Somethin' felt off this time. Somethin' felt wrong, and wouldn't you know it, all of a sudden one hundred Japs jumped out from behind the trees and started shootin' up the place.

The Americans fought back and ended up winnin', but they was trapped. There were only five of them left; they had no food 'cause their boats 'ad been destroyed, and they didn't have much water either. So they were stranded. Now Private Winsor was one of those five, but he had been shot at the base of his spine in the fight and couldn't move his legs at all and on toppa that, the gun fire had made him go deaf. In the unmovin' silence he started livin' in his head. Becomin' more and more detached from the other men.

The days went by and they all started to feel the horrible sting of starvation. Then one day, Winsor went truly crazy and decided that'e wasn't gonna take it no-more. So 'e propped'imself up against a tree, took'is revolver from its holster, and shot the other four men dead. He then crawled over to their bodies, and with'is knife'e carved 'em up. He ate their bodies and drank their blood. In few days help arrived and rescued Winsor. The rescuers discovered the bodies and when Winsor got back to America he was thrown in jail, but quickly escaped.

He was on the lamb for so long that eventually President Truman pardoned him. So Winsor stopped runnin' and settled down; right in this very town. In that house!" James exclaimed, pointing at old man Winsor's house down the suburban road.

The neighborhood children, with dirty faces from playing stick ball in summer's dusty streets, had been listening to James intently as he recounted the story his older brother had told him the night before. They roared with laughter when James swore, and they shook with fear when he described old man Winsor's cannibalism.

They usually hung on his every word despite the fact he was younger than most of them, and this time was no exception. Their ears were hungry for his words, and this story was the story they would remember forever, this was James' best story. By the time James had finished telling the tale, the sun was setting and all across town one could hear the sounds of fathers whistling and mothers ringing bells to signal their children home.

All the boys dispersed, and James was left alone in the street. He started to walk home even though he had not been called in. He was a young man destined for great things. Tall for his age, handsome, and charismatic, the boy was a natural leader among the gang of neighborhood hooligans.

He walked with his head down so that his raven-black hair could fall in front of his glowing green eyes. He liked the sight of his hair swooshing back and forth in front of his face, but more than that he liked the sound of his shuffling feet on the old and crumbling asphalt. Suddenly, something interrupted that sweet sound. A small voice, barely more than a whisper, came from behind James:

"How'd 'e do it James?" startled James tightened up and turned around swiftly. Standing behind him sort of just lingering there as if he were a leaf on a branch of a tree fluttering in the wind was the shimmering gold haired boy from James' class named Winston.

"What'd you say?" James lashed back, quite irate from being startled: "You scared me you know! I hate being scared! I oughta knock your lights outs! I oughta! Now go on speak up! What'd ya say!?"

"I sez, how'd 'e do it?" Winston said again louder.

"How'd who do what?" James snarled.

"Old man Winsor, how'd 'e get outta jail an'all. I mean bein' crippled an' deaf an' all. It musta been mighty 'ard fir 'im to get out an'all. How'd 'e do it?"

"I don't know alright! 'E just did! Okay?" James replied.

"But that doesn't answer the question! How'd 'e do it?"
Winston said now becoming irritated also.

"I told you! 'E just did! Does it matter anyway? I mean the point
is 'e eats people and 'e lives over there an'it's all very terrifyin'!"
James shouted making wide and largely exaggerated hand
gestures.

"It does matter! 'Cause if one part don't work then the rest of
it don't work!" Winston said throwing his arms into the air.
James raised one eyebrow (a talent he was very proud of) and
replied inquisitively:

"What are you sayin'?"

"I'm sayin', I don't think the story is true!"

"Now you just hang up a moment here, are *you* callin' *me* a
liar!?" James snarled taking a few threatening steps forward. With
one hand on his hip he emphasized his obvious outrage by first
jabbing Winston's chest with his finger then jabbing his own and
then Winston's again. Winston shoved his hand away and spoke
defensively:

"I dunno, maybe I am, an'you got no rights touchin' me!" "I
got all rights touchin' you! You're callin' me a liar!" James
shouted inches from Winston's face. Winston gave James a
forceful shove and spoke rationally:

"Now just calm down! I said *maybe I am* I didn't say I
was." "It's the same thing!" James interrupted viciously.

"No it ain't! Who told you that story? Maybe you ain't lyin',
maybe ya just think whatcha sayin' is the truth when it's not."

"Well my brother Richard told me that story, and callin' him a
liar is just as bad as callin' me a liar! Maybe even *worse*!" James
said this knowing that his older brother probably was lying. The
story was probably just a way for Richard to scare him before bed
and give him nightmares (it had worked), but he had to defend
his own honor and the honor of his family from the likes of
Winston Angelus. He knew that Winston's family was "poorer
than dirt", and even though his own family was not much better
off there was no way he was going to let Winston get away with
these kinds of accusations.

"You think your brother would really tell you the truth! He
was probably jus'tryin' t'scare you!"

"Nuh-uh! He told me himself it was the truth! Crossed his
heart, hoped to die, stuck a needle in his eye! He wouldn't lie to
me or nobody ever!"

"He ain't that great and you know it! I heard he gave you a hand full of mud and told it was chocolate and you believed 'im and ate it and then puked your brains outs! And I also heard he kicked the tar out of you last Monday night fir touchin'is radio!"

"What!?" James yelled, red at the face, "Who told you that!?" "Molly Shannon"

"How'd she know that!?"

"Her sister told'er"

"How'd'er sister know that!?!"

"Your sister told'er."

"Well… I … that's… that's just a big lie! A big, fat lie!" James was madder then mad now. Red at the face and breathing deeply he growled: "Alright, you don't believe my story? Then how about this: Tonight, we go to old man Winsor's house and find out."

"Whatcha meanin'?" said Winston with a puzzled expression upon his face.

"I'm meanin' what I'm sayin'!" barked James.

"How's goin' inta his house gonna prove anything?"

"Well… I suppose if 'e really eats people, then there oughta be body parts and stuff in 'is fridge!" James said massaging his chin.

"Huh… I suppose you're right… if he does eat people he *ought* to have body parts in his fridge…" Winston's words trailed off and he shuddered before continuing: "It sounds awful dangerous. I mean if… if! He is a cannibal like you's sayin' it'd be awful dangerous for us to go int'is house."

"What are you? A chicken!? 'E's in a wheel chair! We can out run'im!" teased James.

"Hey! I ain't no chicken, so don't you be callin' me one!" Winston shouted furiously.

"Well you certainly talkin' like one! So! What'll it be? You comin' or not?"

"Yeah, I am comin'." Winston muttered these words. He was not convinced that it was a good idea, but he was not going to let James Kerberos, a boy known as a "fatherless hooligan", call him a chicken.

"Alright… you got a clock in your room?" James said, gazing down at the dirty road in an attempt to avoid making eye contact with the setting summer sun.

"Yeah," Winston responded

"When it reads two in the mornin', you sneak outta y'house and meet me right here. Has y'r daddy got any tools?" spoke James raising his eyes to meet Winston's "

Yeah, he's got tools. Ain't your daddy got any tools?" Winston smirked devilishly. James just glared at him; his green eyes shone for a moment with nothing but peer hate, but he managed to hold it in and utter through clenched teeth:

"Bring a hammer an'a
screwdriver." "Why?"

"Just do it!" James snapped

"Okay, okay! Two in the mornin', screwdriver, and 'ammer. Got it!"

"You better be here!" James barked, taking a threatening step toward Winston.

"I will." Winston replied firmly. It was at that moment that Winston heard the sound of his father whistling and shouting, "I gotta go now" Winston said and as he did the boys could hear James' mother calling as well.

"So do I," James said, "Two in the mornin'!"

"Two in the mornin'!" the boys turned away from each other and headed to their homes for supper.

***

When James arrived home there were four plates set at the Kerberos family dining table. As James entered the door his mother shouted over her shoulder at him from the stove:

"Wash up! Supper is ready!" he walked to the bathroom of the ranch style home that was composed of four rooms (a bathroom, a kitchen, a bedroom for himself and his older brother, and a bedroom for his mother and older sister). After washing up, he found his place at the table and waited quietly to be served, Kraft Dinner and hotdogs.

"I have to work tonight so dinner was quick guys" his mother said. It was the same thing she said every night, but it was not a lie. After this statement was made the family ate in complete silence. After supper, James went to his room and played with his plastic toy soldiers for awhile until an idea struck him. He scurried to the garage and was pleased. He walked back to his room, now ecstatic about the adventure he would embark upon later that night. After his mother had gone to work, James laid in his bed, just waiting for time to pass. When the clock struck half past midnight James' brother, Richard, stood up.

"Richard, what are you doing?" James whispered.

"I'm goin' out. I thought you were asleep. Don't tell mom. If ya do I'll feed you t'old man Winsor! Now go to sleep!" Richard replied. James just smiled relieved that he no longer had to just sit still and count the seconds until two o'clock. Instead, he paced and planned. Talking aloud to no one, he spoke as if he were a great general preparing his troops for a battle of historical proportions. At ten till two he snuck down the hall, past his mother and sister's room to the door that accessed the garage. He grabbed the instrument that was now crucial to his plan and made his way to the front door. He then escaped into the night.

***

When Winston arrived home there were four plates set at the Angelus family dining table. As Winston entered the door his mother shouted over her shoulder at him from the stove:

"Wash up! Dinner is ready!" he walked to the bathroom of the ranch style home that was composed of four rooms (a bathroom, a kitchen, a bedroom for himself, and a bedroom for his parents and baby- sister, with whom he would someday share his room).

After washing up, he found his place at the table and waited quietly to be served. Boiled potatoes, carrots, onions, celery, and cabbage from his mother's garden (there would have been a slab of corned-beef for everyone, but the price of meat had gone up that week).

As they ate they went around the table and each described the events of their day (except of course for baby Christine, only twelve months old). Winston's father told of his day at the factory where he worked on an assembly line everyday with quickly and steeply vanishing hours.

His story that night was about how Chris Shannon fell asleep on the job, and the foreman came down and scolded everyone. Winston's mother talked about how the McHale family had got a brand new television set that was, as she said, "a complete hassle to dust." She continued by saying: "I'm glad we don't have one of

56

those monstrous things! Awful hassle to dust no matter the size and they'll rot your brain mister!" pointing her fork at Winston.

When it came to be Winston's turn he was not sure what to say, but he did not want to lie to his parents. He decided to tell them all about playing football and stickball, and about getting a popsicle at Greg Clark's house (for which they gave him a stern look), but he thought it best not to tell them about the story James told or the conversation that followed.

After dinner he went to his room and waited. He tried to read the tattered book he owned but was too anxious, so he sat there wide awake mentally preparing himself for the evening's coming activity. He did not believe old man Winsor to be a cannibal, but he was still scared. It was well known that old man Winsor was a recluse, but surely he was not a monster, Winston thought, surely not.

When the clock in his bedroom read ten till two, Winston got out of bed and tip toed down the hall through the kitchen and out to the garage where he grabbed the hammer and the screwdriver that James had asked for. He snuck back through the house to the front door and escaped into the night.

***

"James?" Winston whispered in the dark, "James?" he had only the light from the waning crescent moon and the stars, for there were no street lamps in the boys' neighborhood, "James, are you there?"

"Yeah, m'over here!" James whisper-shouted in the blackness, "You bring those tools I as'ed for?"

"Yeah, I got them ri'here, but what's that that you got?" "Is'a saw"

"Whatcha got a saw for?"

"You'll see" James smiled his teeth shining bright in the moonlight, "Now c'mon, le's go!" the boys ran without a sound through the neighborhood. There was a complete rush of adrenaline that washed over them like great waves on a craggy shoreline as they ran, so they ran faster, and even let slip a few anxious giggles. When they reached the sidewalk in front of old man Winsor' house they came to a halt. James put his figure to his lips as a sort of shushing signal to Winston before speaking: "We had better go in the back door."

"Why?"
"'Cause we don't want no one to see us do
we?" "It's two in the morning!"
"Someone could still come by! Now, c'mon!"
James barked quietly, and led Winston around
to the backside of old man Winsor's house. The
boys crept up the decaying wood stairs of old
man Winsor's back porch. Winston did so
backwards, for he was keeping a look out for
anyone or anything that might spot them.
Because of this however, Winston did not see
that they had arrived at the door and
continued walking, in turn ramming James in
to the door.
"Ouch!" James whisper-exclaimed, "Whatcha do that
for?!" "I di'nit mean it." Winston whispered
apologetically
"Gimme that 'ammer and screwdriver!" James whisper-
snapped. He snatched the tools from Winston's hands. "Take
this" he handed Winston the saw, "Step-back" he said pushing
Winston back a few feet. He put the screwdriver into his pocket,
spread his feet shoulder length a part, and raised the hammer
above his head. With a grunt he brought the hammer down as
hard as he could. Blind luck would have that in the pitch-
blackness the hammer actually made contact. He swung again but
missed. The next two times he swung (using all of his force in
each swing) he made contact, and the door knob broke off.
Winston was overcome with panic. The sound of the hammer
hitting the door knob seemed to be the loudest noise he had
ever heard, but nothing stirred. No dogs barked, no birds flew
away in fear, and no one came to investigate. James took the
screwdriver and wedged it into the locking mechanism and
pried it free. He gave the door a slight nudge and it swung
open.
The boys stood there staring into the abyss that was the interior
of old man Winsor's house. Winston spoke:
"Lucky 'e's deaf." Winston said. James looked over at him
and inquired:
"What?"

"I mean if it were anybody else they'da heard us makin' all that noise." Winston met his gaze. James just nodded looked back at the open door and stepped in. The house was understandably darker inside and smelled musky. The boys blindly stumbled around at first, but as their eyes adjusted they could make silhouettes of furniture. They appeared to be in the dining room for they could just make out a table. On top of which Winston could see the outline of a small spire. He handed the saw back to James, and then he cautiously walked up and grabbed the small tower. Bringing it loser to his face for investigation he spoke:

"Just what I thought!" Winston said reaching into his pocket.

"What? What is it?" James asked. Winston just ignored him and carried on. James was about to speak again when suddenly there was light coming from Winston's hands. Winston brought the match up to the candle he had found the table and the room was illuminated. James spoke: "You 'ad matches?"

"Yeah"

"Why'd you bring matches?"

"In case we found a candle"

"Oh…Look there's the fridge!" James pointed toward the humming machine. The boys scurried over to the refrigerator. Once there James grabbed a hold of the big silver handle and looked at Winston and spoke: "Are ya ready?" Winston just swallowed and nodded. James opened the door.

"Oh my God!" Winston gasped. James just smiled. The candle illuminated the inside of the refrigerator. Its racks were stocked full of human limbs, jars of eyeballs, butcher paper labeled "human liver" and "human heart", and glass bottles of blood. Winston stood perfectly still with a horrified expression across his face. James was grinning ear to ear when he spoke:

"I's right!" he looked at Winston who returned the glance before continuing, "C'mon! I got a plan!" James grabbed Winston by the arm and led him through the house. He did not know where he was going but he knew what he was looking for and it was only a matter of time before he found it. He opened every door in the house, checking every room.

The last door he opened was the one he had been searching for. Winston had no idea what was going on. He wanted to leave. He wanted to get out. He only knew that he was in the home of a cannibal, which to him was the same as being in the den of a lion. He was more scared than he had ever been in his life, but when they entered that room it got worse. When they entered the room he first heard the sound: snoring. Next he saw where the sound was coming from: old man Winsor, asleep in his bed.

"No! No! James! No! We have to get out of here!" Winston was frantic. He tugged at James with his free hand.

"Stop bein' such a scardy-cat!" James said shrugging Winston's arm away, "I told ya! I got a plan."

"What kinda plan?" Winston said shaking in fear.

"I wanna see if we can trick'im!" James said with a devilish smirk. "Tr-tr-trick 'im how?" Winston stammered

"Set the candle down over there and grab'is leg!" James directed

"Wh-what if'e wa-wakes up?" Winston said taking a step back, "What're you gonna do anyways?"

"'E's deaf and can't feel nothin' b'low 'is legs! Now just set the candle down and hold 'is leg still for me!" James yelled. Winston saw that old man Winsor did not stir when James was shouting, so he followed directions. He walked over to the bedside. James pulled off the comforter that lay peacefully atop old man Winsor's lifeless limbs, and Winston grabbed a hold of the leg just below the knee.

"No, not like that! Put one'and above the knee on'is thigh and one b'low'is knee like this!" James grouched and Winston followed orders. Old man Winsor's leg was thin and fragile even under Winston's small hands. James placed one of his hands next Winston's on old man Winsor's shin, and used his other hand to raise the saw and lay it to rest just above old man Winsor's ankle.

"What are you doing!?!?" Winston screamed, throwing his hands into the air.

"This is the trick! I wanna see if'e'll eat 'is own foot for breakfast!" James said.

"You're crazy! That's sick!" Winston shouted.

"Don't be callin' me crazy!" James shouted back

"I'm leavin', and I am tellin' on you!" Winston said and started to walk away. James stepped in front of him and growled:

"No you ain't. These are your choices Winston Corbin Angelus: Either you help me do this and we see if 'e'll eat 'is own foot for breakfast, *or* I'll see if 'e'll eat your *head*" James grabbed Winston's t-shirt, pulled him in close, and put the saw blade up against his neck. Winston closed his eyes as tears flooded his cheeks and whimpered:

"Alright! Alright! I'll help you! Please! Just, please don't kill me!"
James released him and they went back to the positions they had
been in before. James began to move the saw back and forth
causing crimson blood to spill out of old man Winsor's leg.
Winston saw this and immediately felt the vomit make its way up
his throat and out his mouth. While Winston closed his eyes and
sobbed uncontrollably, James ignored him and focused on sawing
through the leg. It took what felt to the boys like an eternity for the
foot to become completely free from old man Winsor's body.
Winston now found himself out of tears and his stomach empty.
His crying was just wailing and his vomiting was just dry
heaving. He released his grip on the rest of old man Winsor's
leg, when the foot was free, and looked at James, who was
smiling.

"Finally!" James said with a laugh, "C'mon le's go!" with the
saw in one hand and the foot in the other hand, James dashed out
of the bedroom. Winston looked at old man Winsor who was still
snoring sound asleep and then looked at the blood stained sheets.
He pulled the comforter back over old man Winsor and left the
room silently.

Winston stood in the entrance way of the kitchen holding the
candle, looking at James who was trying to perfectly frame the
foot in the center of the refrigerator. Winston spoke softly but
with a tone that was full of hate:

"I'm leaving"

"What?" James turned around with a desperate look
of disappointment.

"I'm leaving. I'm going home." Winston started to walk to
the back door.

"You don't wanna see if 'e eats the foot?" James inquired with
a tone of surprise as if he were slightly taken back and
offended.

"No." Winston whispered enraged. He set the candle down on
the table as he made his way out the door but stopped just
before he left when James spoke:

"Okay… well just remember what I said," he stated sullenly.

"What's that?" Winston said looking at him with a hint of
confusion and fear in his voice.

"If you tell anyone, I'll kill you." James spoke calmly and coolly
with a blank expression. Winston just held eye contact with James

for a few seconds that felt like a few hours before nodding his
head and taking his leave from the house.

***

Winston never again spoke to James. He never found out if old
man Winsor ate the foot or not, and he did not want to find out. He
never told anyone what they had done. He went home that night,
and lay in his bed motionless and sleepless, just staring blankly at
the ceiling above. He did not cry; he did not speak. There was not
even a solitary thought that ran through his mind. It was as if the
violent fits he had experienced back at old man Winsor's house
had washed away all of his mental capacities.

Winston grew up, and as all childhood events do, the act
committed on that night became a memory, then a heavily
exaggerated memory, then possibly a dream, then definitely
a dream, and then finally forgotten. And one day all the
horrible things that transpired that night may as well have
not have happened, for there was no one left to say that they
had.

The End.

Nothing

John G. Bartell

Physician: Dr. Lotherton
8715-AED19

We go through your garbage cans at night, when you're sleeping. We eat your leftovers. We take the clothes that you couldn't be bothered to donate to the Salvation Army. In the morning you don't know we've been there.

We go through your car. You leave it unlocked because you live in the suburbs, in a nice neighborhood, one with an association, and so you don't have a crime problem. But we're there, at night, stealing your change, your pens, your tissues. You left your cell phone on the passenger seat last Friday night. We didn't take it. We don't want you to start locking your doors. But remember that fancy two hundred dollar pair of sunglasses you think you lost last summer? I'm wearing them.

We'll take your children. You're protective of them, but we're always watching, waiting for you to let your guard down. If you need to stop and get milk, you stop at the gas station and you're just running in and you don't feel like the hassle of getting your kid out of the car seat, dragging her into the store, then getting her back into the seat. You don't think anything will happen to her. You're close to your neighborhood. You have an association. You feel safe, but she'll be gone when you come back out.

We prostitute our teenage children. We prostitute ourselves, but the children make more than we do.

We are everywhere. We are watching you.

One Saturday you'll go into the city. There's an art festival. The wife wants to go, to take your two year old daughter. You want to stay home and watch football on your seventy-eight inch plasma flat screen, but you do what your wife tells you. It's sex night and you can't wait another week.

You're not about to pay five dollars to park in the garage. That's criminal. So you park in your secret spot. You know the city well, you know where to park for free. It's in a nice neighborhood. The streets are lined with trees. The row homes are well kept, the tiny yards are tidy.

You could live there. You have half a mind to do so. To sell the house and move to the city.

There's an alley and you take it because you know the city so well and you know it's a short cut and the sooner you get to the art festival the sooner you can leave and get back home and turn on the big game. So you take the alley. Your wife is hesitant, but you're not worried. It's the middle of the day. It's a nice, tree lined neighborhood with well kept houses. You might even move there.

And besides, you work out every day. You can do thirty minutes on the elliptical without hardly breaking a sweat. So you can protect your family.

It's not so sunny in the alley. It smells like piss. But you're not worried. You work out everyday. Besides, it's a nice neighborhood. It has tree-lined streets.

You grip the stroller and press on.

When you get to the halfway point we send out our first guy. He's scraggly, more so than the rest of us. You're not worried because you figure you can take him. You workout every day.

He smiles as you approach and you see that there is something wrong with him. That this might just be a dangerous situation. Your wife moves closer to you. For a second, a brief second, a thought will flash in your mind. Run, it will say. Get the hell out. But you don't want to show fear. You try to hide it, but it's already too late. We smelled it as soon as you got out of your car.

You pass him, he's looking at you but you avoid eye contact. You think it's ok but he grabs your wife's purse, starts to run. She screams and you let go of the stroller and start after him. You let go of the stroller and run. Let go of your child because your wife's purse is far more important at that moment.

You're surprised to see a man behind you. A big man. You yell *stop him. He stole my wife's purse* but he makes no effort. You say *Man he stole my wife's purse* but he doesn't respond. Instead he grabs your wife's arm, pulls her toward him. You react out of instinct and smash his nose with your fist. It knocks him down. You do three sets of curls everyday at the gym and so you are strong. But you haven't been in a fight in years, not since you were a senior, so you don't kick him when he's on the ground. You don't do anything else. You don't have the killer instinct. You think it's over but it's not. You think you'll just take your wife and kid and go home and maybe call the police and definitely get to watch the big game on your seventy-eight inch plasma flat screen but the big guy gets up. You go to punch him again but he pulls out a knife. A switchblade and he shoves it into your gut.

You go down. It's quiet in the alley. As you fall you see the big guy drag your wife away, hand over her mouth. Her eyes are big, pleading. *How could you let this happen.* You look at the stroller and see the women gathered around it, unstrapping your child. You loose consciousness before they take her away.

When you wake you're in a cinder block room. There are small windows near the ceiling. They let in some light. The room is dirty. You lie on a cot, have a sheet over you. You're cold. Your mouth is dry. You need something to drink. The knife wound hurts but not as much as you think it would. You're cold.

You wonder how long you've been asleep. It could be hours, but it could be days.

The door opens and a policeman walks in.

Thank God you're here you say.

Why'd you kill your family? He asks.

I didn't you say.

Who did then?

Gypsies, you say. *Gypsies.*

I think it was you the cop says.

You can't believe it and you tell them again that it was Gypsies.

They prefer to be called Romas the cop says.

He looks familiar. You wonder if you know him. If maybe he's pulled you over for speeding.

Whatever you say. *You got to catch them.*

He shakes his head and laughs, then pulls out the switchblade and you know he's not a cop. You know how you know him. He flicks it open and drives it toward you but stops before it hits your flesh.

We're not Romas he says.

What have you done with my wife you ask. *Is she alive?*

She's alive he says. *What would you give me for her?*

You tell him anything you want.

Your car he asks. *Your house? Your life savings?*

Anything, you say. *Take it all.*

He grins. *But it's not yours to give* he says.

You say *what do you mean.*

She already gave it to us.

You feel relief. You think your wife has paid your ransom. That you'll be able to leave, to go home, to watch the big game on your seventy-eight inch plasma flat screen.

She gave it to us so that we would free your daughter.

You hadn't thought of her. Only of your wife. And yourself.

He walks out of the room. You hear the door lock.

You're naked and you're cold. You pull the sheet tighter. It stinks in the room. Your cot stinks. The sheet stinks but you're cold so you cling to it.

Your eyes grow accustom to the dark and you can see the stains on the sheet. There's dried up cum on it but you don't care. You're cold.

After some time, you don't know how much time, the door opens and a woman enters. Her face is wrinkled. Her hair is dirty but well combed. She looks to be fifty but is probably thirty. She carries a tin cup.

You been asleep for three days now.

I'm awake now.

We was wondering if you was alive.

I am you say.

We was wondering.

You ask for some water. She gives you the cup. A dead fly floats in it. You filter it out with your teeth. The water tastes dirty. Tastes oily but you want more.

Can I have some more you ask.

Do you want to fuck me she asks.

You say *no, I want my wife. Where's my wife?*

I bet you do want to fuck me.

Do you have any more water? You ask.

Do you think I'm ugly? Is that it? Is that why you don't want to fuck me?

She is the most offensive woman you have ever seen, but you tell her she's pretty, that you would fuck her. Under different circumstances. And you ask her for some more water.

You think you'd get one for free? Don't you. That's how you people are.

You think maybe I'll fuck you for free.

She sounds mad. You're cold. Your wound doesn't hurt as bad as you think it should. You want something to drink. You want your wife. You want your child.

What would you give me to fuck you right now she asks.

You don't answer because you don't know what to say.

She pulls the sheet back and looks at you. You're naked. A napkin is taped to your wound.

You got nothing to give me she says and drops the sheet back onto you and walks out.

You beg for more water but the door slams shut.

You lay for a period of time. You don't know how long. You think you will be able to judge time by changes in the light coming through the windows but the light seems constant.

You are cold. You think of your family. You hope they are safe.

Your wife comes in after a period of time. An eye is swollen. Her lips are swollen. Her hair is dirty but combed.

She looks at you once then never makes eye contact again.

You tell her how happy you are to see her then you ask her if she called the police. She shakes her head and doesn't say anything.

Did you?

It won't do any good she says.

We have to you say.

I tried.

We need to tell them.

I went there she says, *to the station. They said I was crazy. They told me to leave. I stayed. I begged them.*

She stops talking.

What'd they say you ask.

A captain took me to a room. He smashed my head into a desk. Told me to leave. That they have real crime to worry about. That he better never see me there again.

You don't believe it. It seems like a dream but it's not. You're cold. Your wound doesn't hurt as bad as it should but she doesn't ask about it.

You ask about your daughter. Your wife tells you she's living with her aunt.

Let's go you say.

Where? she asks.

Let's go get her you say.

She explains that you're not allowed there. That the aunt thinks you're bad parents. That you shouldn't be around your kid. That she'll call the police on you.

Well let's just go you say.

Go where she asks.

Go home.

We have no home. They took it from us.

We'll just go somewhere you say. You're starting to get mad at her. As if it's her fault. Your wound doesn't hurt as bad as it should but she doesn't ask about it.

You don't have any clothes she says.

You tell her you'll call your boss.

You don't have a boss she says. *Or a phone.*

You just stare back at her.

You were fired. You can't come on the property. They'll arrest you.

You want to know why but don't have the energy to ask.

Do you have any water you ask.

She doesn't.

You ask her if she brought you any clothes. She didn't.

We got to get out of here you say.

To where? Were will we go she asks.

Can you just get me some clothes you ask. You're starting to get mad.

I don't have any money she says.

You say *use a credit card.*

You don't get it she says.

You're thirsty. And now you're hungry. And you're cold.

Can you just ask someone for some money? you say.

They want things she says. *For the money.*

It takes a moment but you understand. You wonder if she has already done things for money. If she goes to bed hungry.

I need some clothes you say.

I'll go she says and starts for the door.

You don't have to do this you say. You don't really mean it and she can tell so she leaves. She doesn't say good-bye, she doesn't say I love you. She doesn't ask about your wound.

You're cold. Your mouth is dry. And now you're hungry.

Come back you say but you know she can't hear you.

You picture her on the street. You're cold. You hope she hurries back.

Some time passes and now the light is starting to dim.

You need a drink of water.

You fall asleep. When you wake nothing has changed. It may be darker but you're not sure.

Your mouth is dry. It seems like it's taking your wife a long time.

It's quiet. You tap your finger on the cot. You're cold. Your wound hurts but not as much as it should. You wonder what kind of clothes she'll bring to you but then you realize it doesn't matter. She's not coming back. You have nothing to offer her.

You're cold. Your wound hurts. But not as much as it should.

The End.

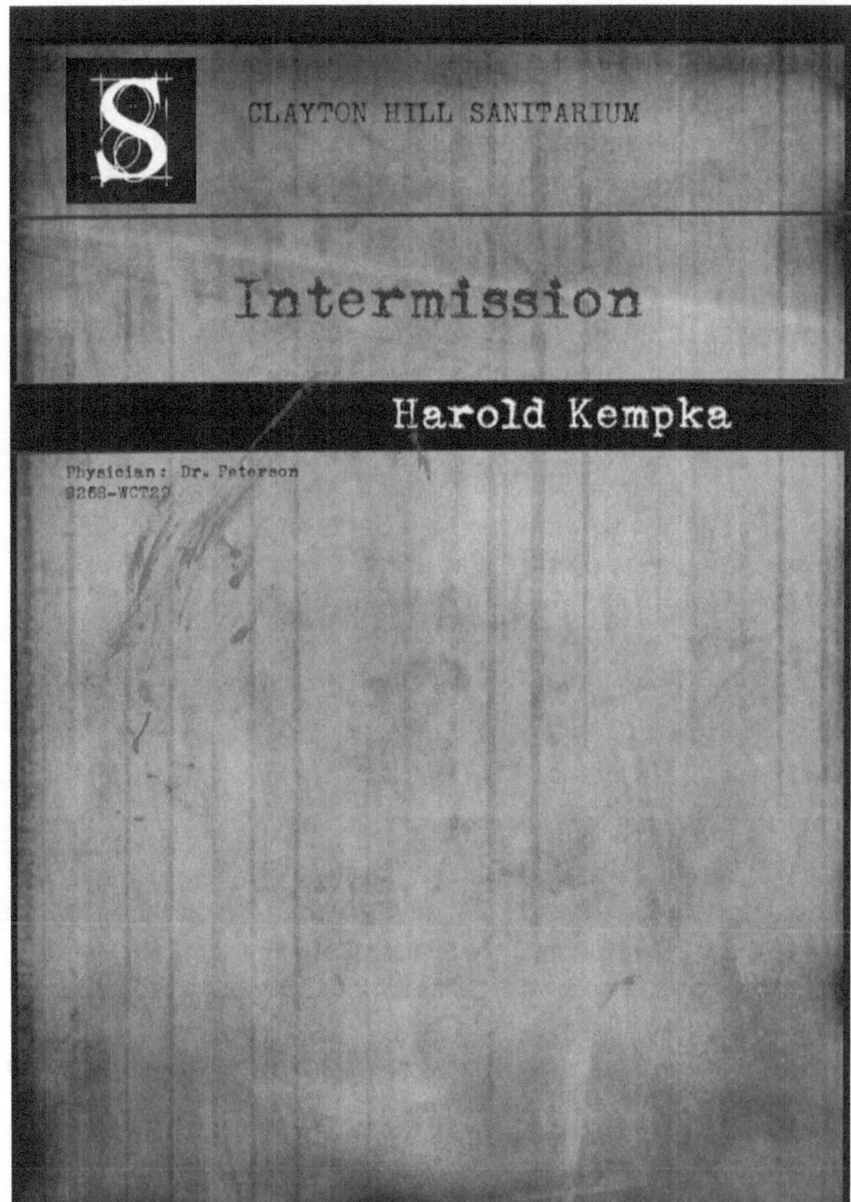

CLAYTON HILL SANITARIUM
Intermission
Harold Kempka
Physician: Dr. Peterson
9268-WCT29

The lean, pasty-faced young man grabbed a cart at the drugstore entrance and darted inside. As he disappeared into the cosmetics aisle, Blanche the cashier waved to him. "Morning Richard, how are things at the house?" He stuck his arm over the top, and waved back. "Fine, ma'am. Mother says hello."

"How is Myrna?"

"Well, we've both been fighting a nasty bout of pneumonia. She's still recuperating, but you know what a trooper mother is."

Several minutes later, he stepped up to the checkout counter. Richard set shaving cream and new pack of razor blades on the belt, followed by his mother's favorite makeup items, fragrant candles, and cleaning supplies.

"Are you still acting at the playhouse?" Blanche asked.

"Not recently, though I did audition for a new play, and they told I would probably get the part."

"Well, good for you. Listen; tell your mother I might come by for a visit later today."

"I will! Let me know what time and I'll tell her. You know how vain she is; she always wants to look her best, even when sick."

"You're such a thoughtful son."

"Well, if I didn't get all this stuff done," he said with a shrug, "mother would never let me hear the end of it."

After swinging by the post office to pick up the mail, Richard stopped at the bank to deposit her monthly Social Security check.

***

After completing her shift, Blanche drove over to see Myrna. A neatly manicured lawn and colorful flowerbeds lined the sidewalk. She silently praised Richard for his meticulous work ethic.

After knocking several times, the door opened a crack and Myrna peered out from the shadows.

"Well, hello Blanche," she rasped, covering her hacking cough with a handkerchief. "Richard said you might stop by. Please come in."

As she stepped inside Blanche replied, "He certainly is a good son. Is he home?"

"No, he wanted to be here but had to leave to help a friend at the last minute."

Slivers of dusty sunlight slid between the drawn shades, illuminating the otherwise dark living room. The floral aroma from the candles Richard bought intermingled with the living room's stuffy warmth.

Myrna hobbled into the room, and sat on the couch clutching her afghan across her shoulders. She motioned Blanche in, but she remained at the door.

"Listen dear; you still look a little under the weather. I'll come and visit another time."

"A-h-h, a little thing like a cold won't keep me down. Besides, I don't get company very often."

"No, you rest. Have Richard make you some soup when he comes home."

After Blanche left, Myrna went to the kitchen, and cut up the last of a leftover rump roast. She mixed some in with the cat's food, and set the bowl on the floor

"Here kitty, dinner's ready."

That evening, Myrna draped a shawl across her shoulders, and took her weekly walk to church. She sat in the back pew. After a short bout of coughing just before communion, she declined to partake and left before the service concluded.

Once home, Myrna poured a cup of brandy. She added a little honey to help smooth the rawness in her throat, and descended the cellar stairs.

***

Richard sat at a dressing room makeup table he had made, and removed his mother's wig. He set it on a mannequin head, and then glanced into the mirror smirking. His mother's facial pelt immediately puckered and separated from the adhesive on his face.

He carefully peeled it off and draped the expressionless mask over her plaster, facial cast. Richard turned and opened a nearby freezer. He removed his mother's frost-covered head and gazed into her cloudy, colorless eyes.

"I am so excited mother. I have accepted a role in a play at the theater. Playing you has been quite daunting, and I need a break. Now don't worry; I'll tell everyone you are visiting relatives out of state."

He set her head back in the freezer next to her neatly labeled and packaged remains.

"Oh, and in case you were wondering," he continued, "Kitty and I are eating well."

Richard closed the freezer lid, and climbed the steps to make a sandwich from the few remaining slices of her rump roast.

The End.

Pretty Things

Luke Tarzian

Physician: Dr. Lichten
6428-SED41

"Don't you want to be like us—don't you want to be a pretty thing?"

She nods enthusiastically. They're so beautiful, so majestic and pristine. Their smoothness captivates her and she wants to be with them—to be *like* them.

"Then you must throw away the ugly, rid yourself of what is old and broken. Do away with all that's rotten, for we'll never speak of it again."

She takes the razor from the counter, staring hesitantly.

"Don't you want to be like us—don't you want to be a pretty thing?"

She nods and starts the transformation at their urging. The razor slips and slides, cuts and saws, and soon the mass of hair is gone, resting in a pile at her feet. She looks at them enthusiastically— they cock their flawless heads and ponder: "Perhaps if you cut here and there, shave a little more…don't you want to be like us—don't you want to be a pretty thing?"

Once again she nods and sets to work, cutting here and there, shaving off a little more. The mass of hair that falls is doubled, resting at her feet, a pile ankle-deep. She looks at them inquiringly, the razor shining in her slightly shaking hand.

"Am I pretty now?" she asks, and winces slightly as some crimson liquid drips between her eyes.

"You're so pretty now!" they laugh. "You're just as beautiful as we are—let's ask the others what they think!"

And so the others rush into the room, staring through the magic two-way mirror, laughing scornfully and pointing: "Look at her— she's *such* a pretty thing!" They laugh and tease some more. "She's such a pretty thing!"

The pretty things inside the mirror cackle and remove their pristine faces, mocking her with emerald eyes and long blond hair, flaunting rubber countenances—holding "pretty faces" in their hands.

"Now you're just like us!" they jeer—"Now you're such a pretty thing!"

And then they vanish in a flash, their frigid teasing, taunting, laughing resonating through the room. She's crying now, as blood streams down her face. It trails between her eyes and drips off of her nose, collecting and congealing in the mass of hair around her feet. She cries and cries, she tries to put it back—but the hair will not hold place, for it's not fit for such a pretty face.

On the mirror's other side their taunting still persists. They laugh and joke at her expense and call her nasty names: "Oh what a stupid girl she is—to think she's just like us! Hairless, horrid Mary—bleeding like a fool! Bloody, stupid Mary—she's as pretty as a mule!"

Mary's parents find her on the floor, a scarlet-painted razor in her hand, glistening wickedly in the bedroom light. Her eyes have been destroyed, mutilated by the blade, and leak some foul and pus-like substance, while the many trails of blood congeal along her face. Beside her is an ugly mound of hair, an open laptop, and a note: *I'm such a pretty thing—and soon they will be too.*

***

The blond ones with the emerald eyes surround the laptop in their room, cackling like crows. They stare with pompous glee at their reflections, doing up their hair and dabbling with their over-priced cosmetics.

"We're all such pretty things!" they sing—"We're all such pretty things! Hairless, horrid Mary—how she wishes she were us! Bloody, stupid Mary—she's as pretty as a mule! Bloody Mary! Bloody Mary! Bloody Mary! *Blood*—"

And their bodies hit the floor—their perfect hair falls out in clumps, and pus and gore burst from their gnarled and mangled eyes, blemishing the floor.

"Now you're just like me—now we're all such pretty things!"

The End.

Zombie Apocalypse Now!

Rachel Tsoumbakos

In The Beginning....TATIANA

The stars were bright and winked at me knowingly. I scowled and tried to ignore them as I blew smoke rings. Each circle perfectly sailing through the last. It had taken me weeks to get the hang of it. But now I had all the time in the world for things like that.

Tap-tap-tap-tap.

Instinctively I rose and made my way back inside. It was so nice up here on the roof, in the dark. It felt safe. I'd shimmied down the metal ladder and was half way across my lounge room before realising that that wasn't a john at the door, it was a goddamned zombie. How they managed to make it up the narrow staircase, I could never work out.

While inside, I decided not to make it a wasted trip and pulled another beer out of the bathtub. There was no hot water and no electricity now, so cold water and the tub were the only way of chilling beer now. Passing the kitchen, I also scrounged through the barren pantry. It was a choice between spam, tinned tongue and a packet of Easter eggs I'd found wedged under one of the aisles in the supermarket. I'd eaten one egg the day I'd found it, the chocolate was all mottled with age, but it still tasted good. I pushed aside the treat and pulled out a tin of tongues. While it wasn't appetising, it was all that was left in the store now.

The stars. I never got sick of the stars now. I stayed up all night (through habit and my trade) and slept all day. The nighttime was now my only friend. It was so lonely now, I even missed my clients; even the sickos.

The zombie continued to butt against the door. It made me miss the old times. All the crazy, funky things this apartment had seen. I smiled, wishing, for about the thousandth time that there was still a stash of weed behind the statue on the mantle. At least there were still cigarettes. Maybe for not much longer though. The shop two doors down only had a couple of cartons left and the last one I'd bought back was dry and stale.

The beer was good. I drank half of it before attempting the tongues. The rest of the beer was good for getting rid of the taste of the meat afterwards. Lighting the last cigarette in the packet, I realised if I wanted those last few packets of smokes, I'd need to get them tonight. While zombies didn't seem to sleep, their sight seemed to be better in daylight, so it was less risky to travel by night. Not that scurrying over the rooftops and shimmying down drainpipes posed much of a risk in the zombie department.

Standing on the very edge of the roof, I peered down over the town I'd come to know as home. It was black. Mostly. In three spots, I could see the glow of life. Two people had candles burning. The gentle flicker bounced off the walls of their confines. The other light was more consistent. Maybe a battery operated lantern? Every night I watched these signs of life; the signs of the living. Once I'd called out,
But no one heard me. Or no one listened anyway. At the same time I threw my cigarette butt over the edge, one of the candles was blown out.
I sighed and went to get ready.
Pulling on a pair of old leggings, I caught my eye in the dusty mirror. I scratched at my hair and decided it was time to try and work out how to get into the chemist from the roof. Three inches of regrowth was just not acceptable! I could live without acrylic nails and foundation, but once a blonde, always a blonde.
I tugged on my camo high-heeled boots. I'd bought them two years ago to go with some matching shorts. There was a john who liked his women all military, I was happy to oblige; kinky role-playing paid better after all. Who would have known they would turn out to be so hand during the apocalypse? Checking the heels, I noted I hadn't cleaned all the zombie brains off from the last time I'd staked one through the noggin. Gross. I really needed to clean that once I returned. I wasn't sure how contagious the virus was, so there were no taking chances.
Pulling the two-toned hair back, I wrapped a tie once, twice, three times around it and reached for my lippy. It was habit. If I couldn't have colour in my hair, it had to be on my lips. Grabbing a large tan satchel, I swung it over one shoulder and across my body. Inside it was a torch and a kitchen knife.
"Taaaaaattsssss.....!"

What the fuck?

I whipped my head around, towards the moan. Did that zombie just say my name?

My heels clicked on the floorboards as I marched to the door.

The sound seemed to enflame the zombie.

"Tiiiiiiittsssssss.......Taaaaattssssss.....!" It was followed by a strangled moan.

I felt ill.

There was only one john who used to like to make fun of my name.

"Peter?"

The word was out before I even realised I'd thought it.

Silence.

Tip-toeing, I carefully made my way to the front door. There was a little peephole there. I leaned over and pushed aside the red cover. The sight was gut-wrenching.

"Heeeelllllpppppp....meeeee....." his voice trailed off. He thudded his head against the door.

"Pete, you know I can't let you in," I replied softly.

I sat down at the foot of the door, my head resting on the cool wood. The tinned tongue was threatening to reappear after seeing Peter. How could he change so much? He'd always been handsome. So good looking in fact, that I couldn't understand that first time, why he needed a hooker. Then he explained what he liked and I understood. Most girlfriends won't change a grown man's diaper.

"How long have you been like this?" "Nnooooo..."

I wasn't sure what he meant by that. So I kept talking. "Honey, I am going to open this door, okay?" "Ttttiiiiiittttsss.....?"

"Yeah, baby, you can see Tat's tits," I replied. The tears were threatening. "You can have a real good look. But only looking, okay? No touching?"

"Uuuuuhhhh....." That was probably a yes. It didn't matter; I was too busy wiping snot and tears on the bottom of my black singlet. One last sniff and I stood up. Peeping out the little window, I could see Pete as he shuffled from one foot to the next. Oh my god, he was feeling himself! I shuddered and swallowed back the tinned tongue.

"I'm opening the door now, Pete," I said, turning the lock. I tucked my bag behind me, not wanting to give him something to grab onto.

Pete was silent.

"You still there honey?"

"Uuhh...huuuuh..."

"Okay, Pete," I replied. The tears had returned. I sobbed once more. It was a wretched, choking sound. I eased the door open.

The zombie formally known as Peter stood as still as the statue I hid my weed in.

Not looking a gift horse in the mouth, I lunged at him.

My aim was true, even as I hobbled on my one remaining high heel. The other shoe was now protruding from the middle of Peter's skull.

He looked surprised. And then sad. Finally, he crumpled to the ground.

I pulled my shoe out quickly and swiftly slammed the door shut, locking it.

"Fucking zombies," I muttered.

READ THE NEXT INSTALLMENT OF "ZOMBIE APOCALYPSE NOW! IN ISSUE 005

Dear Sanitarium,

I have written my first draft for a novel and I have read and re-read it over the last 6 months. I think it is ready for release but do you think I need to hire an editor?

Lucy,
Norfolk

Once piece of advice that has stuck with me as a writer is always take longer editing thank you think you need to. Once you release it and people start reading it, if there are plot holes, spelling or even formatting mistakes your first impression is not great. So I would spend time and find an editor that works in your genre and don't hire the cheapest. Good luck with your novel.

Dear Sanitarium,

I spend a lot of my time browsing old book stores and I love the look of old cloth covered books. With eBooks you just can't get that look or texture, or not that I have seen. Do you have any ideas of cover designers that offer this?

Melvin, Little Rock,
AR

Well that is quite a specific look you are going for. I too am fond of that cover technique, so I did a little digging. There are a few websites that have scanned these types of books, allowing you to see the texture, which you can use as a template for your cover. Searching for "book cover texture" brings up a good selection of such sites.

Dear Sanitarium,

I have written a handful of stories and I am happy with them apart from the titles. I just cannot seem to come up with one that stands up well. I have tried one word titles but I just end up with nonsensical titles that lack punch. Other times I try long titles in the style of M.R James but again that just seem trivial. Do you have any suggestions or tips?

Greg,
London

Some people will tell you titles will make or break a story. Just like a poor cover will be glanced over, but get it right and people will be shouting your titles from the rooftop. If only it were that simple. Titles are a hard thing to master, some of our writers don't come up with the title before the story is written and then it comes to them organically. Others will start with a title and go from there. I would re-read the story and think about how it makes you feel, is there a part that sticks out? Brainstorm around those feelings and items – you might surprise yourself.

Dear Sanitarium,

First off I must say I love your fresh approach showcasing new horror fiction. I am not a writer; I just devour as much horror as I can get my hands on. As such your top 10 has put me on to several new authors, so thank you for that (my purse is a little lighter each month though.) My question is; are you going to have any themed or special editions out next year?

Julia, Greytown,
SA

Thank you for your comments we are so blessed to have writers such as the ones in this month's issue, along with the previous contributors who want to share their work with us. With regards to themed editions, it is something that we are talking about in the office. So watch this space.

Dear Sanitarium,

I have started working on my own author website, I'm a complete novice and was wondering if there is an easy way to get up and running?

Jerry, Santa Ana, CA

There are several different options for an easy "set up and go" approch to creating a website. Wordpress.org, blogger, wix.com and weebly.com are worth a look if you don't want to code your own site. We have had this question a few times, so we will be doing a feature on it soon. In the meantime have a look at those websites mentoned and let us know when it is live.

LETTER OF THE MONTH

There are several different options for an easy "set up and go" approch to Why is it the Horror genre has had a resurgence in the film industry, but the fiction side is still in the minority when it comes to shelf space in bookstores? I have to travel to the next town over as it is the only bookstore still open, only to find one small bookcase for the horror section. It does have the latest bestsellers but after that it's mainly King, Hill, Koontz and the like. All great writers but i want something more. Keep up the great work bringing us new and exciting writers each month.

Yvonne,
Germany

It's such a shame to hear about the lack of horror available. In a small way that's why I'm glad so many talented writers self-publish or send their work into magazines like ourselves. At least that way we are able to try new works without much fuss. Hopefully bookstores will wake up to this and stock a greater selection sooner rather than later. creating a website. Wordpress.org, blogger, wix. com and weebly.com are worth a look if you don't want to code your own site. We have had this question a few times, so we will be doing a feature on it soon. In the meantime have a look at thosewebsites mentoned and let us know when it is live.

"Overheard in the Office"

"Hopefully a Kindle Fire HD will be under
the tree this year.'"

"Krampus!"

"They are having a fire sale! - shipping $40 -
nah i'll leave it. "

"New iMac's are out...must fight urge"

"Why isn't there ever a strain of skipping
zombies?"

Top 10

Bestselling US Horror

1. The Remaining: Refugees by D.J. Molles

2.Into the Hollow (Experiment in Terror #6) by Karina Halle

3. Priceless (A Sexy Urban Fantasy Mystery) by Shannon Mayer

4. Last Stand of the Dead (White Flag Of The Dead) by Joseph Tal-luto

5. The Christmas House by Barry KuKes

6. Branca dos Mortos e os Sete Zumbis (Portuguese Edition) by Abu Fobiya, Deive Pazos and Eduardo Spohr

7. The Neighbors by Ania Ahlborn

8.After Dawn (Book 3 of the Into the Shadows Trilogy) by Karly Kirkpatrick

9. NIGHT CHILLS: A Bracken and Bledsoe Paranormal Mystery by
Bruce Elliot Jones and April Campbell Jones

10. Snowblind by Michael McBride

Compiled Nov 1st - Nov 30th
2012 Amazon.com Kindle Chart

Top 10

Bestselling UK Horror

1. Cold Days: A Dresden Files Novel by Jim Butcher

2. The Remaining: Refugees by D.J. Molles

3. Last Stand of the Dead (White Flag Of The Dead) by Joseph Tal-luto

4. Containment (Alaskan Undead Apocalypse Book 2) by Permuted Press and Sean Schubert

5. Into the Hollow (Experiment in Terror #6) by Karina Halle

6. Mineral Hunters (Space Exploration Part 2) by Matthew Hawk-ing and Situjuh Nazara

7. The Peeling Trilogy by Iain Rob Wright

8. Ritual by V L Young

9. Out for Blood (House of Comarre) by Kristen Painter

10. The Fall of Society (The Fall of Society Series, Book 1) by Thonas Rand

Compiled Nov 1st - Nov 30th 2012 Amazon.co.uk Kindle Chart

Group
Therapy
12.12
A Zombie workout, an age
old question and a new
convention planned

Get Fit. Escape Zombies. Become a Hero

That is the tagline for Zombies, Run! The application available on iOS, Android and Windows Phones. It started life out as a Kickstarter campaign which is where I first came across it. I just missed out in pledging towards it but now it has been out for a little while and the features they have added have really improved its appeal.

The game puts you as Runner 5, a survivor living in the township of Able. Each mission or "run" allows you to enhance the story, pick up supplies for the township whilst avoiding running into zombies. Over all there are 30+ missions, "zombie chase" interval training sections and you can play it with your own music whilst you run. A new feature Six to Start have added is you can use it on the treadmill – not the best way, but none the less if the weather is crappy you can still get your zombie fix on.

Now the gamification of fitness regimes has boomed over the past 18 months, with the likes of Runkeeper and Fitocracy to name a couple. But this does it really well – the story seamlessly runs along and you find yourself wanting to hit the streets again and again to unlock new items and missions.

The app is quite pricey however, coming in at £7.99 (£5.49) and with a download of just under 400MB - you better have a wifi connection to hand. Looking past the price you can see a lot of love and effort has not only gone into the initial creation of the app but the aftercare is second to none. New missions have been added, a 5k training app has been released and now they have included "Zombielink".

Zombielink syncs your running, music and mission data and puts it all into a online management system. You can track previous runs with distances and speeds and you can even playback past mission audio if you missed anything. This feature is being used by the community to help runners with their fitness and even music choice.

I cannot get over the level of polish that this app has achieved and

I have a feeling it is only going to get better.

Zombies, Run! By Six to Start
Cost: $7.99 / £5.49
https://www.zombiesrungame.com

It's an age old question; what is scarier Zombies or Werewolves?

That is the premise behind a new game that is on Kickstarter. Created by Chuck D Yager to answer a 12 year old argument this game is now ready for release. The video for the campaign starts off quirky enough but soon shows a simple "round of play" and I must say for a quick 2 player game (15 minutes-ish) it seems like a fun game.

I don't think I've every asked that question before but now I am starting to see both sides of the argument. Slow shuffling threat (Romero camp) Vs only out on a full moon etc.

The game has you trying to scare 6 randomly drawn citizen cards that are community cards. From there you take turns laying down cards to try and reach a scare factor that is higher or equal to that on the citizen card. Once you have done that you take the card and keep it in front of you.

You do this until all 6 cards are claimed; add up the points that are on the citizen cards and the player with the most points win. You can counteract and place bonus cards but for more information check out the videos.

The artwork is great and has been self-funded by Yager – this is the second time he has run this campaign. However this time the overall target is lower than the one previous. At $1400 he is hoping to get a small print run together and with the campaign running until the 4th Jan I think he will do it.

The opening reward level of $25 gets you a copy of the game (Int order need to add $10 more), but for $30 you get the special edition with limited edition box art – signed by the game designer. The top tier reward lets you be a citizen in the game – not a bad touch for only $150.

Zombies Vs Werewolves
End Date: Jan 4th 2013
Target: $1400

We're bringing Lovecraft back to Providence!

A kickstarter campaign has begun to bring a premier convention to the area of Providence. - H.P Lovecraft's hometown.

This convention will be running over three days from 23-25 August 2013.

Over those three days they will be covering topics such as Literature, Science and Exploration, History and Culture. The organisers are confident that this will easily be the largest gathering of Lovecraft aficionados ever - and you can be part of it.

The reward level you will be interested in is the $100 level. This will get you the three day pass, a t-shirt, a sigil jewel pin and a sticker pack and a few other download goodies. Loftier reward levels will also get you VIP access to the Horror Film festival run by Arkahm Film Society - ran the weekend before NecronomiCon.

As you read further down the rewards you quickly get a sense of the level to detail the organisers are going for. From the location to the sigil pins. Everything that is included has a purpose and a meaning to all Lovecraft fans.

The campaign runs until January 9th and is looking to raise $16,000. With backers joining daily I don't think this will be one to fail.

So if you are into Lovecraft and want to spend a few days with people who "get you" you could do worse than back this campaign at the $100 level.

NecronomiCon: The Premier Lovecraft Convention in Providence
End Date: Jan. 9th 2013
Target: $16,000

On the .
Record

We are joined this month by
Author Carrie Green.
Carrie has been writing since she
was five, influenced by her
grandmother to carry on her
talents. Carrie has now released
three books, two are a collection
of short stories and one a
novella.

Thank you for spending
some time with us.

*With writing you must have
seen a few trends come and go in
the writing world. What ones did
you think would die a death but
haven't?*

Actually, few people are aware of how long it took for eBooks to
arrive. I can recall over ten years ago when the first eReaders
(clunky and heavy) were produced and people were
experimenting with online books (Stephen King, famously, issued
one) to be read on PCs. All the media at the time thought that it
was a long shot and that eBooks would never compete with
printed books. I was as sceptical as anyone. I actually
downloaded King's book and gave up after printing the first few
chapters—I ran out of ink and I didn't enjoy reading a book on a
computer screen. I didn't see how it would catch on…

*With that in mind which ones do you think have had their time
and should bow out gracefully?*

Trends come and go. The worse crime would be when people
write copycat versions of the latest bestsellers. I've given up
reading anything labelled as YA as they usually turn out to be
weak imitations of the Twilight series. Try to find your own
voice. The hottest trends actually sprung from originality, which
is the reason why these manuscripts usually faced multiple
rejections from publishers (as in the Harry Potter series).

As mentioned you have written a novella and short stories, is there where your heart lies?

I love all forms of writing, even poetry, but I acknowledge that the novel is the most commercial format, if you're seeking writing success. I use short stories and novellas as promotional items to be given away free or cheaply to introduce my writing style to the general public before my first novel is released.

On your website [carriegreenbooks.com] you mention that you love the freedom that horror gives to the writer as there are so many aspects that you can bring to a story. What is your go to subgenre when you have a little downtime and just want to experiment with characters?

I honestly always write horror/thrillers, it's just the way my mind works. In reading, my selection is rather broad; I'll read any genre, if a book captures my fancy. I have a secret enjoyment of comedic romances, but I'm not likely to write one.

Some writers like to set their stories in areas they know; do you have a set location in mind for your stories?

Usually I select Midwest locations as that is where I'm from and my knowledge of the area adds creditability to the fiction that I'm spinning (the best lies have an element of truth).

If you could go to a location for research purposes for a story, where would you go?

I do go to locations for research purposes when writing important scenes, and for tax purposes, I'd like to state that these are spas, expensive restaurants, and exotic vacation destinations.

Speaking of research and travelling. Do you have any items or gadgets that you just have to have on you at all times to help with your writing?

My PC, a dictionary, and a thesaurus. I write and edit directly on the computer, due to learning how to write in this manner for PR. It's faster. When I first starting writing it used to be in long-hand and then I typed it. Back then I carried a little notebook, but today all I have with me is my phone. I have, however, taken photos on my phone that were meant to help me recall a certain setting.

You are a big user of Twitter and you tweet almost daily. Do you tweet on a whim or do you plan your tweets?

My Twitter campaigns are a combination of monthly scheduled tweets via HootSuite and spontaneous tweeting when I have a spare moment. You really need both to produce an interesting stream of tweets.

Staying on Twitter you do tweet a lot about other writers and their works, which is great. Do you find those writers thank you or ReTweet you a lot?

There is an amazingly supportive writer community on Twitter. People RT my tweets all the time and I try to return the favor. I also have writer friends that I've met through Twitter, blog tours, and book launches; and we will exchange promotional tweets on a regular basis.

You are a blogger as well not for just your site but also for the World Literary Cafe (http://worldliterarycafe.com). How did that come about?

I wrote the press releases for Melissa Foster's 'Come Back To Me' and for the World Literary Café. She invited me to blog on the WLC site and I was pleased to contribute and help other writers out in the complex process of book marketing and publicity. In my day job, PR, I was responsible for promoting several traditional business books from major publishers, but I'm learning, along with everyone else, how to promote eBooks.

On those blogs you offer some great advice for writers, what one piece of advice where you given that has stuck with you?

In regards to Social Media, select the platform that you most enjoy and stick with it. Too many writers are spreading themselves thin, trying to do it all. You don't need to participate in every form of

Social Media. Experiment, see what clicks for you.

It can be Twitter, Facebook, YouTube, Pinterest, Google+, Goodreads, WordPress, various forums, etc., but it won't be all of them. Know that fact going in. You need to leave time for writing.

Investigate free or inexpensive tools to make your Social Media easier, faster, and more productive. A simple Google search will turn up lots of tips and suggestions. Social Media can become a full time job, but writing should be your full time job. Don't lose sight of the big picture.

Do you have any advice for our readers?

Right now there are tons of free eBooks being offered—read them. It costs nothing but a little time. If a book sucks, stop reading it and move to the next one. There are some great authors out there. Once you find an author that you enjoy, please support them by buying their other books. Additionally, a thoughtful review is always appreciated!

And finally if you had a portrait taken with you holding your favorite horror book, what would it be?

Wow, I have to select just one? Hmm, since it's a photo, I'll select 'Carrie' by Stephen King, as it's sort of ironic. It's my first name and I'm sure that it's the novel that most people think about when they see a horror author named Carrie. I want to be your prom date, hee,hee… Hide the knife set, hee, hee…

Thank you to Carrie for sharing her time and thoughts with us, and if you want to check out Carries books be sure to head over to her website or check her out on Amazon.

www. carriegreenbooks.co
m   www.
worldliterarycafe.com

Where the Horror Happens with Joe Mynhardt

We are delighted to be joined by Joe Mynhardt – owner and founder of Crystal Lake Publishing. It is a small press operating out of South Africa. They publish horror short story collections and anthologies in both eBook and Print from.

So what is your workspace like?

Unfortunately, quite small. As a teacher in my day job (that's whenever I'm not playing superhero behind my laptop), I live on the school premises in a small flat with my wife and two dogs. My office space consists of a small desk-like table with my laptop, external hard drive, lamp and a small trophy I received from a local writers' association here in my hometown of Bloemfontein – inspiration is key. I'd love to say there are no distractions, but the kids run around upstairs and the bell rings constantly. Oh, and my dogs don't like it when I neglect them. One great thing about this situation is absolute silence during the holidays, and the ability to completely shut myself off from the rest of the world. I'm sure that'll always be a good skill to have.

Do you have a go-to gadget / app or service that you cannot live without?

I'm addicted to my laptop and Kindle, and physical books of course. Let's not forget my portable Wi-Fi thingy. Winamp also works well when I'm editing or running errands on the internet, but not when I'm writing. Right now Eric Clapton is wailing away on one of his many guitars.

Do you have a set routine while you work?

I'd love to say I finish my writing before I go on the internet,

is my goal. I just can't relax and concentrate on my writing while there are emails left unanswered. I've never liked the idea of making people wait. Hopefully I'll get there some day, but for now, my routine goes something like this: Switch on the laptop. Stare at whatever scary background I chose for this week. Check my three email accounts (one personal, one for my writing and the other for Crystal Lake Publishing), try to spend as little time on Facebook as possible, then it's off to Mywriterscircle (where I'm a moderator), and three other forums I frequent. Then I jump off the internet as quickly as possible, before I get any funny ideas.

Most writers prefer to never write and edit at the same time, but I have to edit a few pages before I can continue writing a story. Not only does it help me focus on the project, but it gets me into the frame of mind I was when I wrote the previous section, and keeps the pace and mood of the story in check with what went before.

What is the best piece of advice you have ever received?

Always be professional, approachable and as helpful as possible. We're all extremely busy people (can't wait to hire a PA some day), but that gives no one the right to be rude or snobbish when it comes to networking. Being a writer, editor or publisher is a profession, and should be treated that way at all times. I think the exact quote, not sure who said it originally, was, "Just be professional, dammit!"

Be professional, dammit! Couldn't resist. How's this: Never give up. Write. Write. Write. Read. Write some more. It's a tough business, and it doesn't get easier, ever, but damn it's fun. Worth every second, every grey hair, every bald patch.

Meet other writers, read their work, discuss it with them, be polite, help them, thank them, check what they did to get where they are now.

The bottom line is, if you present yourself as a professional and do your absolute best every day, people will not only notice you, but they'll respect you.

If you would like to read more about Joe and Crystal Lake Publishing you can find them on Facebook or their site.

"Lost In The Dark" available from Amazon and For the Night is Dark is set for release early 2013.

We hope you enjoyed this issue of
Sanitarium Magazine.

If you have any feedback or would like to leave a review please
head over to Amazon and share your thoughts about Sanitarium.

Thank you for your time and we salute your
love for all things horror.